Make You Mine Again

"I guess I'm too late, since you have moved on."

"You're right, it's too late and there is no need to go rewriting history and pretending there's a future between us."

Bradley stroked her cheek. "You never answered my question."

She wanted to succumb to the tingles his touch sent rushing though her body. "I—I don't have to," Jansen said, then snatched away from him. "I'm going to my hotel. Alone." Bradley grabbed her arm.

"So, you're willing to settle for safe? Willing to have a life without love..."

Unraveled

"You were here, right here, exactly when I needed you. Meant to be. What is that?"

"I heard somebody call it fate before."

"Fate and I are going to be friends if it's got my back like that." Ona raked down her hair as a surge of wind stirred it. After a few moments of combating the breeze, she gave up the fight. "Why are you watching me?"

As his hands cradled her face, she thought that he might kiss her again. But his fingers moved up to rake her wind-tossed bangs back.

Cheris Hodges was bit by the writing bug early. The 1999 graduate of Johnson C. Smith University is a freelance journalist and always looks for love stories in the most unusual places. She lives in Charlotte, North Carolina, where she is trying and failing to develop a green thumb.

Books by Cheris Hodges

Harlequin Kimani Romance

Blissful Summer with Lisa Marie Perry

Visit the Author Profile page at Harlequin.com for more titles.

Lisa Marie Perry has received high praise from *USA TODAY* and has been nominated for an *RT Book Reviews* literary award. She lives in America's heartland. She drives a truck, enjoys indie rock, collects medieval literature, watches too many comedies, has a not-so-secret love for lace and adores rugged men with a little bit of nerd.

Books by Lisa Marie Perry

Harlequin Kimani Romance

Night Games
Midnight Play
Just for Christmas Night
Mine Tonight
Blissful Summer with Cheris Hodges

Visit the Author Profile page at Harlequin.com for more titles.

Blissful SUMMER

Cheris Hodges
Lisa Marie Perry

HARLEQUIN® KIMANI™ ROMANCE

ISBN-13: 978-0-373-86411-9

Blissful Summer

Copyright © 2015 by Harlequin Books S.A.

The publisher acknowledges the copyright holders of the individual works as follows:

Make You Mine Again
Copyright © 2015 by Cheris Hodges

Unraveled
Copyright © 2015 by Lisa Marie Perry

PLEASE RECYCLE · THIS PRODUCT IS RECYCLABLE

Recycling programs for this product may not exist in your area.

HARLEQUIN®
™ www.Harlequin.com

Printed in U.S.A.

CONTENTS

This book is dedicated to
anyone who has loved, lost and found true love again.
Love is worth the risk and a second chance.

Dear Reader,

Sometimes your plans for the woman you love don't match up with her plans. Jansen and Bradley loved each other, but she wanted to spread her wings.

What Bradley didn't understand was that she needed his support and his love. He also didn't understand that no other woman could ever take her place.

I hope you enjoy Jansen and Bradley's story and have as much fun reading it as I did writing it.

You can follow me on Twitter, @cherishodges, like me on Facebook, or email me at cheris87@bellsouth.net.

I look forward to hearing from you.

Cheris Hodges

MAKE YOU MINE AGAIN

Cheris Hodges

Chapter 1

You are cordially invited to celebrate the union of
Miss Shelby Elaine Stephens
and
Mr. Jacques Luc Renard
Saturday, the 25th of April,
at half past three in the afternoon
at the Shangri-La Hotel Paris

Jansen Douglas smiled at the invitation that arrived to her photo shoot in Harlem, but her smile quickly turned to a frown when she realized that attending Shelby's wedding would more than likely mean seeing her ex-lover, Bradley. Talk about a blast from the past, a painful memory that the years and her success as a model hadn't erased. But, whatever. She wasn't going to miss Shelby's wedding! She simply had to meet the man who'd been able to tame the young Miss Stephens.

Shelby had a reputation that spanned the East and West coasts as a love-them-and-leave-them type of chick. Of course, some of the stories had been wildly exaggerated. Like the one about her and an A-list superstar and the fact that she had been the reason for movie star Ian Kelly's trip to rehab.

Shelby and Ian had starred in a movie together that bombed at the box office, but their exchanges on social media made it seem as if they had something else going on.

After the movie failed to launch Shelby's career, she decided to move from being an actress to living off the trust fund that she had received from her family. Some people called her a professional party girl. She, however, was simply a woman of leisure.

This didn't make Bradley happy at all, since he thought Shelby should've been working with the family business.

Unlike Bradley and Ian, she and Shelby had remained close over the years. The one rule to their friendship: never mention Bradley. But she knew that he was going to be front and center at this wedding.

So, she thought as she filled out her RSVP card and added a plus one. She'd planned to be in Paris this spring. She'd had five years of being "the Face," an international top model. But over the past three months, her bookings had declined and she noticed a decrease in the fees she commanded. Granted, she was still making a hefty salary, coming in at number two on a recent *Forbes* list of top-paid models, but her accountant did tell her that her income had dropped ten percent.

It was a good thing that she didn't spend as extravagantly as many of her colleagues in the industry.

"Jansen," the photographer called out. "We're ready."

Smiling, she glanced down at her rainbow silk dress from the new collection of Branford Diaz, and then headed to the studio and took her mark. Photographers loved Jansen because she didn't do the diva thing, even though she was well within her rights to do so. Instead, she took direction, criticism and ended up with fabulous pictures. She'd been the favorite model of some of the top photographers, according to industry rumor.

"I'm ready," Jansen said with her trademark smile.

Bradley Stephens, CEO of the Stephens Family Resource Center, was two seconds from screaming. Shelby, his younger sister, was getting on his nerves with this wedding that she was supposed to be paying for, though he'd just received a stack of bills from France.

"Yancy," he said, calling for his assistant. The comely blonde walked into his office and offered him a cautious smile.

"Yes, sir?"

"Please do me a favor, remind me that when my sister gets married, she will no longer be my problem," he said then shook his head in anguish.

"I'm sorry," she said with a shoulder shrug.

"Yancy, have you gotten the contract from the catering company about the banquet for the girls?"

"Yes, they just arrived. Let me get them," she said.

"And then you can take the rest of the day off," Bradley said. "I appreciate all the work you've done for this banquet."

"I just wanted it to be a success as much as the last one was," she said as she walked out of his office.

Bradley paused. The banquet had been the brainchild of Jansen Douglas. She had been the one who'd suggested that the foundation have a celebration to thank the donors a few years ago. They'd been wrapped in each other's arms in bed that night.

Her skin had been as smooth as silk as he'd stroked her arms while she laid out the plans for the event.

Memories of Jansen Douglas always made him shiver with regret.

Bradley quickly busied himself with a report of the financial reports for the foundation's first quarter. Private donations were down fifteen percent and that gave him pause. He wondered if he needed to funnel more money into marketing the foundation or if he should follow the Kickstarter trend to get the new shelter in Atlanta funded.

One thing he knew for sure, this wedding wasn't going to be the multimillion-dollar event that his sister had dreamed up in her head. Shelby was quite frivolous and he needed to rein in her spending. And he knew it wasn't going to be long before he had to deal with his bean-counting brother, Kenyon, who would be griping about Shelby's wedding. Though Bradley had been surprised that it had even gotten past the invitation stage. His little sister was a bit of a commitmentphobe. He couldn't blame her. Love was about sacrifice. Something he could write a book on. But, at the end of the day, if Shelby was going to settle down, it would be worth not reading about her exploits in the gossip rags. Glancing at a picture of his parents, Bradley smiled. They were either laughing or shaking their heads in heaven at their three children.

The car accident that took Joan and Winston Stephens haunted him, shaped him, made him afraid to give his all to anyone because he couldn't handle losing her. The way he'd lost Jansen. Slamming his hand on the desk, he didn't have the time or energy to get lost in emotions or the past. He had to call his sister and tell her that her fairy-tale wedding was about to be too much for him to pay for. It wasn't that he didn't have the money; she just needed to realize that there were more important things to do with three million dollars.

Jansen washed the makeup from her face and sighed. Photo shoots were starting to get tiring, but the runway was still her first love. "Jansen," her assistant, Dove Lace, said as she walked into the washroom. "Donovan Strange just called. He wants you to meet him for drinks tonight."

"Finally," she exclaimed with a smile. She'd been trying to meet with him for three weeks.

"Said he'll meet you at the Flatiron Lounge around eight."

Jansen glanced down at her Burberry watch. "That's less than two hours from now." She frowned, then nodded. "If you don't mind, call him back and tell him I'll be there."

"I already told him that you're available. He's so handsome."

Jansen rolled her eyes. Handsome men were a dime a dozen and she wasn't looking for love—not ever again. Not that selfish kind of love that meant she had to turn her dreams off to make a man happy. Closing her eyes, she chided herself silently for allowing Bradley to slip back into her mind. She was supposed to be so over that man, but every now and then he'd rear his handsome face in the rearview mirror of her mind. Men from all over the world had romanced her. But in her heart of hearts, she knew no one could take Bradley's place. And she hated that she compared everyone to him. An egomaniac, lovable and deliciously sexy man who made her hot just thinking about him—after all this time.

Yes, Donovan Strange was handsome. He was also one of the most powerful names in the fashion world. He'd designed some of the hottest gowns and red-carpet looks. Stars like Beyoncé, first lady Michelle Obama and other A-listers sought him out when they needed a one-of-a-kind look. His work had been highlighted at Fashion Weeks in Paris, Milan, New York and Los Angeles.

He was known just as much for his business acumen as he was for his designs. Jansen wanted him to help her transition from model to model agency owner. There were things that Jansen wished she'd known about the fashion industry before that day in Lenox Mall.

With Donovan's help, she hoped to open a full-service agency for models to groom them for life in front of and behind the camera. She hated that the stereotype of models was beauty and no brains. Jansen had fought it her whole career. There had been plenty of people who'd underestimated the fact that she had a master's degree in public policy and had experience with a world-renowned nonprofit agency that helped women and families. Sometimes she missed that work. Missed doing more than just lending her face and donating money to groups that did what the SFRC did. And even though her relationship with Bradley had ended badly, she still supported the center and its mission. There he was again, in her head. She needed to get her game face on because she had business to attend to. She picked up her bag and headed out the door. When Jansen saw a car waiting for her, she wanted to kiss her assistant for saving her the hassle of hailing a cab in the sweltering spring heat of New York. Hopping into the air-conditioned car, she smiled in relief. As she was about to lean back and close her eyes, her cell phone rang.

"Yes?" she said when she answered.

"Ooh, someone is in diva mode."

"Shelby! You have a nerve. Besides, I'm channeling my inner Shelby. Girl, I'm just hot and tired."

"Yeah. I heard it's steamy in New York, but here in Paris, it's a cool sixty degrees."

Jansen sucked her teeth. "Just rub it in, heffa. So, tell me about this man who actually got you to say yes."

"We can talk about that this weekend. I'm flying in to New York to get some ideas for my wedding dress."

"Baby, you're in the fashion capital of the world, why are you coming to New York?"

"Great, then you'll come to Paris." Shelby sounded like a kid asking to get picked up from camp early.

"Negative. I have another photo shoot in a few days, and then I have… Wait, why do you want me to come to Paris?"

"To talk me out of this wedding." She said it breathlessly, as if she'd been holding it in for weeks.

"Shelby, why do you need anyone to talk you out of getting married? Your lovely invitations have already been sent out."

She sighed and Jansen couldn't help but wonder if her friend was getting married to satisfy her family—more specifically, Bradley. She groaned inwardly, there she was thinking about that man again.

"What if I love him more than he loves me?"

"Why do you feel that way?"

"Because of you and Bradley."

"Ugh! I'm going to hang up on you."

"I know we're not supposed to talk about *that*, but

you gave him everything and what did you end up with?"

"Think about your parents," Jansen said. "They loved each other unconditionally."

Shelby groaned this time. "You know our generation doesn't roll like that. I'm not trying to get married and then find out that the man I love is screwing around on me or…"

"That never happened with me and Bradley. I'm just saying."

"Jacques is amazing and beautiful. But the French are different."

"Honey, you're different. You're the kind of woman who a man can't get over. You're overthinking it."

"Or maybe I didn't think enough. I'm always jumping into something headfirst. That's it, I'm calling the wedding off."

"Girl, that's crazy and impulsive. Why did you agree to marry him if you had such doubts?"

"Because I love him. I'm just being crazy and your favorite Stephens is driving me nuts. He had the nerve to tell me that I need to tone my wedding down. Hello, it's Paris. Over-the-top is expected."

Jansen marveled at how Shelby went from canceling her wedding back to planning it in a single bound. "You're my favorite Stephens."

"Sure, if you say so. You know, he's going to walk me down the aisle."

"That's great," Jansen said, trying to keep the sarcasm out of her voice.

"Anyway, maybe…"

"Let me stop you right there. I don't care what your next statement was going to be, I don't want to hear another word about your brother."

"Well, your serial dating only proves that you're not over him."

"I don't serial date."

"Jake Bensimon doesn't think so. I took him off the guest list."

"Whew, thank you so much."

Shelby laughed. "I thought he was going to be the one for about fifteen minutes. He's the reason Jacques and I met."

"And you're not inviting him to the wedding?" Jansen asked, furrowing her brows. "That just seems rude."

"Honey, it wasn't as if it was a good thing. Jake was drunk on the French Rivera and was lamenting about you. He was getting loud and embarrassing, so I kept trying to get away and he kept pulling on my arm. Jacques came rushing over and knocked him out. I love a Frenchman's passion."

"I bet," she replied. "And you want to give that up?"

"Oh, hush. I'm just suffering from cold feet. And… Let me call you back."

"All right, and I can't wait to see you in that great wedding dress." After hanging up with Shelby, Jansen closed her eyes and sank into the leather seats, wanting nothing more than ten minutes of sleep. But all she could think about was how she was going to ignore Bradley when she ran into him in Paris. Then another thought popped into her mind. What if Bradley arrived at the wedding with his new woman?

So what. It's time for us to move on anyway. I'm sure Bradley Stephens isn't thinking about me at all, Jansen thought as she opened her eyes and blankly watched the passing cars.

Chapter 2

"You were talking to who?" Bradley asked his sister as he kicked his feet up on his oak desk.

"Jansen. What do you want, Bradley?"

"How is she?"

"I can't talk to *you* about her," Shelby said. "That's the only reason she's remained friends with me. But if you want to beg for forgiveness, I'll let her know."

Bradley sighed. "Is she going to be in your wedding?"

"No. She doesn't do bridesmaid dresses. I know you didn't call me to talk about my bridesmaids."

"No, I called you because I got these bills. You're spending too much with this wedding."

"What?"

"I'm trying to prevent you from hearing a lecture from Kenyon," he said.

"Fine, I'll take him off the guest list. I know this is about the grudge he's holding because of the—"

"We've had enough fighting in this family and I'm pretty damn sick of it."

He heard Shelby suck in her breath. She had been on Kenyon's side for a while when he wanted to shut down the family center after their parents died. Sure, Kenyon had been a little harsh when he said the center had been their parents' dream and it was time for the three of them to blaze their own path, with a business of his own. Bradley had wanted nothing more than to preserve the legacy of Joan and Winston, who'd established their foundation to protect women who society ignored and turned its back on. Shelby had been a little oblivious to the work that the center did until she discovered that her friend Yancy had needed the SFRC's help to escape an abusive situation. She felt so bad for almost allowing her greed to keep her friend's family from getting what they needed. She'd also understood why Kenyon wanted to do his own thing. But when he'd sued Bradley and the Stephens estates to get his inheritance early, things had gone too far.

For three years, the Stephens were a fractured family. And maybe that had been why Bradley felt abandoned when Jansen followed her dreams, leaving him with someone else's expectations. Part of him resented Jansen because she'd been able to do what he couldn't. Been able to press forward and do what she wanted and not what had been expected of her. But if he'd been totally honest with himself, Bradley would've realized that he'd placed those expectations on himself. And he'd just assumed everyone would've fallen in line behind him.

It had taken a while for the family to recover from the lawsuit, which Bradley had won, and he retained control over the estate. What Shelby and Kenyon hadn't realized until they had gotten their portion of the inheritance, Bradley had been a deliberate steward of their money. All he'd asked was that they'd participate in the annual fund-raisers. Shelby did it happily. Kenyon grumbled, but he did his part, as well.

"You know Kenyon is never happy about anything, I want my wedding to be a happy day," she said. "I don't want to hear him talk about—"

"Shelby, don't be like that," Bradley said, then laughed. "He's just trying to look out for you."

"Whatever, he's hoping that I self-destruct and he gets to pick up the pieces."

"No one wants that to happen. And… Let's just focus on happy, Shell."

"I thought you were calling to tell me to stop spending money. How's that happy?"

"Shelby, I called you because three million dollars is too much for a wedding and the marriage probably won't last a year."

"Why would you say something like that? I guess because you can't hold on to who you love, you think we're all going to have that same issue. You never got over Jansen and can't keep a woman for more than three months. That's your story not mine!"

"Shelby, you're an impulsive hothead. I know this man is either blessed with the patience of Job or he's just as volatile as you are. Why haven't you brought him to Atlanta?"

"So you can give him the third degree? I don't think so. You'll meet him when you come to Paris."

Bradley sighed. "Is he good to you?"

"Do you think I'd marry him if he weren't? I want that end-of-the-world love that Mommy and Daddy had."

The kind of love Bradley had thought he and Jansen would've shared. He'd wanted nothing more than to have her by his side, as the center became a national resource for women and children in trouble. Had he been wrong to think that his plan wasn't the same as hers?

Obviously.

"Hello? Bradley, are you listening to me?" Shelby's sharp voice brought him back to the present.

"Yes, you love him, he's good to you and you're going to bring him to Atlanta."

"Clearly," she said with a laugh, "you weren't listening."

"Kenyon and I want to meet this man, Jack—"

"It's Jacques."

"I bet that dude is from Detroit, moved to France and—"

"This is where I hang up on you," Shelby said. The next thing Bradley heard was the dial tone. Laughing, he hung up the phone then logged on to Google. He was determined to find this guy's Detroit birth certificate. Bradley laughed at himself after he hit Enter. He didn't have to check the guy out; he knew without a doubt that Kenyon had already taken care of it. That dude was more suspicious than a roomful of CIA agents. He thought everyone with a pulse was after money.

Bradley sighed and didn't want to admit that, as of late, he'd been feeling the same way about some of the women he'd dated. Their main goal in life seemed to be the next cast member of *The Real Housewives of Atlanta* as Mrs. Bradley Stephens. As if he'd ever let that happen. "Yancey," he called out, and then he remembered that he'd given her the rest of the day off. Deciding that he wasn't going to get any more work done, Bradley decided to treat himself to an afternoon of doing nothing.

* * *

That Donovan Strange was hilarious ran through Jansen's mind so many times that she could barely get out what she'd needed to talk to him about. He kept her laughing about everything.

"Jansen," he said as he waved for a waiter. "I know you didn't want to meet with me to be bored with stories about your colleagues. What's going through that pretty little head of yours?"

Jansen smiled and waited for the waiter to set another bottle of wine on their table. She folded her delicate hands underneath her chin and smiled at him. "The future."

"The rapper?" he quipped. Jansen frowned, wondering how he made such a huge mark in the fashion industry when he was never serious. Maybe that was his secret. But failure wasn't an option for Jansen.

"You and I both know that my expiration date is fast approaching. Any model after twenty-eight is old news in this industry," she said.

Donovan shook his head and poured himself a glass of wine. "Jansen Douglas, you're the Face. What are you worried about?"

"The next face that comes along. Donovan, I don't want to end up on some reality show faking a marriage."

"Are you kidding?" he asked. Seemingly taking note of the serious look on Jansen's face, Donovan eased back in his seat. "What are you hoping to do, Jansen?"

"When I came into this industry, I didn't know anything and there are a lot of people who like to take advantage of young girls. I want to curb that."

"So, you're thinking of starting a full-service agency?"

She nodded. "I want to help these girls and show

them that they're worth more than what people see on the outside."

Donovan smiled. "I heard that you used to work for a family resource center, I guess that's where you get this desire to help people. What exactly do you need from me?"

"A mentor and access to investors. You are more than an amazing designer, you're a brilliant businessman."

"So, what do you want me to be? The mentor or the money?"

"I'd love for you to be both, but I'm realistic."

"Meaning?"

"Everyone knows the economy has changed, and I can't expect you to just give me money for my start-up."

"But you're smart enough to know that you shouldn't tie up your capital in your start-up. I'm impressed. Do you have a business plan?"

Jansen sighed, remembering why she needed a mentor. "No. I've been doing some research on how to draw up a business plan. But I just have a few paragraphs."

"Let me see."

She pulled her iPad from her oversize purse and opened the file she'd been working on for the past three months. Donovan took the tablet from her hands and slowly read the outline of the plan. "May I offer you a few suggestions?" he asked.

"Please."

Donovan placed the iPad in the center of the table and they huddled around the tablet. He suggested that she tailor the business plan to fit different lenders and investors.

"Just a rule of thumb, I'd create three different plans that say the same thing."

Jansen laughed. "See, that's why I need you."

"What you have here is good," he said. "This has the potential to help empower a lot of models. Both new and veterans… But there are going to be a number of industry folks who won't like this."

She shrugged. "Why not?"

"Because you're trying to empower women to own themselves."

"Why shouldn't we?" she asked with her right eyebrow raised.

Donovan reached for his glass of wine, took a long sip and then smiled at her. "I'm all for it," he said, then raised his glass as Jansen reached for hers. "Let's toast to the success of the Jansen Project!"

Jansen clinked her glass of wine against his and smiled. She felt confident that the Jansen Project was destined for success. Suddenly, flashbulbs went off around them as a pack of paparazzi started firing off questions.

"Are you two dating?"

"Get out of here," one of the bouncers, who was rushing toward the photographers, snarled. With his massive arms, he started pushing the mob forward.

Donovan laughed as he downed his wine. "I guess this is what a date with the Face is like. Not that this is a date," he said. "But I'm sure the blogs will run with that."

Jansen crinkled her nose. "Anyone with a Wi-Fi connection and a keyboard calls themselves a reporter these days. The sad thing is, people believe what they read in the blogs more than they do on legit news sites."

After another bottle of wine, Jansen and Donovan decided to call it a night. They headed out of the club and stood on the curb, waiting to hail a cab. After the scene in the club, the manager took care to make sure there were no paparazzi waiting for them when they left.

"You know," he began, "this meeting came with strings attached." He wiggled his eyebrows and Jansen's stomach dropped. *Was he really one of those guys?*

Taking note of her furrowed brows and narrowed eyes, he grinned. "Jansen, not those strings! I have a show coming up and I need a flawless showstopper. That would be you."

She released a sigh of relief. "I'd love to. When and where?"

"Paris in April," he said. Jansen clapped her hands and smiled.

"That's awesome because I'm going to be in Paris this April."

"Kismet," he said. "I'll email you the details. And just so you know, this will be the debut of my wedding collection."

Jansen's smile faded a bit. She was beginning to wonder if the only wedding gown she'd ever wear would be in a fashion show.

Chapter 3

Bradley drove aimlessly though Buckhead, not wanting to go home but having no desire to hang out at a
club or bar. He hated nights like this. He didn't have
any work to do and he wasn't interested in a booty call,
though he had a few numbers he could dial for com-
panionship. But tonight, his mind was on one woman.

Jansen.

Every so often, his yearnings for her would render
him restless. His mind would always return to those
last moments, the day he ran her out of his life. Bradley could still see that pained look on her face as she
stormed out of his office.

That face. That beautiful face.

"This is how we're going to end things?" she snapped.

*"You walked in here and said you were leaving. All
I said was go."* She hadn't expected this to be the reac-
tion to the news of the lucrative modeling contract she'd

been offered and her chance to spend six months in Italy as she worked with veteran designer Lupe Diego.

"How about supporting me, Bradley." Jansen slammed her hand against his desk. The move startled him, he'd never seen her this angry before. But what was she mad about? The fact that he wasn't doing backflips because she was leaving him? When did she get so caught up in the modeling thing? "Supporting this frivolity? You're beautiful, but so are thousands of women." What he didn't say was that he felt the modeling industry was filled with users who would be using their influence to sleep with novice models like Jansen to get what they wanted.

"Stop."

"What we're doing here makes a difference. And—"

"You selfish bastard. I can't believe you're trying to belittle what I want to do because it doesn't meet your standard of—"

"That's not what I'm saying, Jansen. But the work we're doing here makes a difference..."

"And if my modeling career takes off, you don't think I would continue to help girls and families in need?"

"You're too smart to be a model."

Jansen stalked toward the door. "And I'm also too smart to deal with a man who's so blinded by his own vision that he can't see past it." She grabbed the doorknob, then turned and looked at him. Bradley hadn't risen from his seat. She narrowed her almond-shaped brown eyes at him. "I guess I'm right."

"Trying to let you come to your senses."

Jansen picked up a crystal paperweight and threw it on the floor. "I have come to my senses. I've done nothing but love and support you. Now that I need you, you want to dismiss my dreams! That's rich, because you're always preaching to young women that they matter."

Now he was on his feet, stomping over to her. "Have you lost your damn mind?"

"No, I just found it. All of these years, I put your needs first. Was I supposed to be the clouds and the sun in the background of your damn life? A pretty face for you to show off in Atlanta? I want more and I'm going to get it."

"Don't leave," he said with a bit of a quiver in his voice. "Jansen, I—you know what..." He wiped his hand across his face. "Go. Because I'm not going to be the reason you pout for the next twenty years."

Jansen sighed and squeezed the tears back in her eyes. "Go to hell, Bradley." Turning on her heel, she stormed out of the office and Bradley stood there as if his feet had been rooted to the floor.

Regret stung him today as hard as it did three years ago. He should've gone after her. A horn blared behind him, alerting him to the light change.

Blowing through the intersection, Bradley decided to head to the Waffle House for a hearty meal and strong coffee. Then he'd go home, find some work to do and stop thinking about Jansen. As he stopped at the next red light, he saw a billboard featuring Jansen selling perfume—looking larger than life and more beautiful than he remembered.

Maybe when he saw her in Paris he could do what he should've done years ago—apologize for being a jackass and kiss her one more time.

Jansen loved days like these, no photo shoots, no early-morning makeup sessions, just listening to her favorite playlist as she jogged in Central Park. She still marveled at the sights and sounds of the city. Every day, even after the three years she'd been a full-time New Yorker, she found something new to love.

Then again, she was truly fooling herself. She was still a Georgia peach, but she couldn't and wouldn't go back to Atlanta because she didn't want to be faced with running into Bradley and his new family.

How do you know he has a family? she thought as she slowed her pace. *So what if he does. He probably found a nice subservient woman who does everything he says.* Jansen sped up as a mixture of jealousy and anger pushed her forward. Why did she care? How many years had they been apart? And he never once tried to contact her or personally said thank-you for her yearly donation. Walking to the East Green section of the park, Jansen decided that silence would serve her better than another three miles of running.

What would she do when she saw him in Paris? *Ignore him,* she thought.

After roaming around the park for another hour, Jansen decided to treat her assistant to lunch at db Bistro Moderne. Although she didn't love the place, Dove was enthralled with the bistro. And she deserved it after setting up the meeting with Donovan.

Dove reminded her of many of the girls she'd wanted to help in Atlanta. She wasn't the most efficient assistant in the world, but she worked really hard and was the closest thing Jansen had to a girlfriend in the city.

Befriending models had never worked for her. Everything was a competition and she didn't have time for that madness. That was one of the reasons why she and Shelby remained close, despite what happened between her and Bradley.

"Jansen," Dove said when she answered the phone,

"I could have sworn you said your meeting with Delicious Donovan was a business meeting."

"Well, hello to you, too," Jansen quipped. "And it was a business meeting."

"Not if you read *Hot News*."

Jansen expelled a frustrated sigh. "I hate that website," she said through gritted teeth.

"What were you two huddled over? I swear that picture looks like the two of you were going to kiss at any moment. So, did you?"

"See, I was calling you to take you to lunch, now I'm rethinking that."

"Oh, don't be like that, Jansen. I've had a few calls this morning about you Donovan. I didn't believe it until I saw that picture."

"You know what, I hope no one else believes there's something more than business between us," Jansen said as she nibbled at her lip. She hated rumors, and more than anything else, she loathed that everything she did was newsworthy to some. "You know, if people covered the other things that I do the way they cover who I date… I'm not getting on my soapbox tonight."

"I hear you. But are you going to address the rumor about you and Donovan. And if you don't want him, tell him I'm single."

"Stop it," Jansen said with a laugh.

"I'm just saying. Since I've been working for you, you haven't given anyone half a chance to win you over. Remember that dude who wanted to marry you?"

"Please don't remind me of Mr. Stalker," she said, referring to Jake Bensimon, a man who didn't know the meaning of the word *no*. "Dating him was one of the biggest mistakes of my life."

"But he was a cutie-pie."

"With several issues, let's move on."

"Yes, about that lunch. What time should I be ready?"

"About two? At db Bistro?"

"Sounds good. I'll see you then."

After hanging up with Dove, Jansen rushed home so that she could take a look at the coverage of the nonstory about her and Donovan. No matter what was written, she wasn't going to address it at all. Her personal life, or lack thereof, was her business.

Bradley woke up from a restless sleep to the sound of his phone ringing. "Yeah?" he said when he answered.

"Bradley," Kenyon said, forgoing a hello. "We have a problem."

"Do you know what time it is?"

"Six-thirty, and did you know your sister's wedding is the same time as the gala."

"You're calling me at six-thirty on a Saturday morning to tell me something that has already been taken care of? The date of the gala has been changed to October, and had you read the last few emails that I sent you, you'd know that already."

"All right, that's not why I called you. I just wanted to wake you up to see if you're still holding a torch for Jansen Douglas."

"I'm going to get out of my bed and come to your house to kick your ass. I'm seriously trying to rest."

"Just answer the question."

"Why?"

"I just read a story about her and some dude that asked her to marry him last night."

Bradley sat up in bed as if he'd been jolted with a cannon blast. "What?"

"I guess she's over you. Why did you ever let her get away?"

"I'm hanging up on you."

"All right, all right. But you know what today is, right?"

Bradley glanced at the date on his alarm clock. The accident.

"You want to go have breakfast?" Bradley asked, realizing that his brother would never admit how he was feeling.

"Sounds good to me. Let's meet at the West Egg Café."

Bradley smiled, that was their father's favorite place to take them on Saturday mornings when Shelby and their mother were at the hair salon. "Big brother, are you all right?" he asked.

"I'm really feeling it today, Brad. I thought about the last thing I said to Mama and…"

"She knows you didn't mean it."

"How do we know that?"

"Because Mama would've forgiven you for your outburst regardless. Sometimes it did feel as if she was spending more time with other people's families, but she had enough love in her heart for all of us."

"Yeah, well, I was being an asshole and I never got the chance to say that I was sorry."

"We can go visit her and Dad after we eat," Bradley said as he rubbed his eyes with the back of his hand.

"Do me a favor," Kenyon said.

"What?"

"Don't tell Shelby that I called you this morning being emotional."

"How much is it worth to you?" Bradley quipped.

"You jerk."

"See you in a little bit." Pulling himself out of bed, Bradley took a quick shower and dressed in a pair of black cargo shorts and white polo shirt. As he brushed his wavy hair, he tried not to think about Jansen with another man. Walking back into his bedroom, he opened the nightstand drawer and pulled out the small black box that he'd been holding on to for the past three years. Opening it, he ran his finger across the brilliant five-carat diamond he'd called the Jansen stone. He'd had the ring designed just for her, shaped like a heart, white gold and platinum.

I bet her fiancé went to a freaking chain store, he thought as he snapped the box closed and tossed it back into the drawer. It was time for him to get over Jansen. She'd obviously gotten over him.

Jansen pulled her hat down over her eyes and ran past a horde of reporters and photographers. How did these people always show up at the first sign of a scandal? You'd think she'd been caught kissing President Obama. "Jansen, Jansen," a reporter called out as she jogged to catch up with the model. "Is it true that your relationship with Donovan Strange is the inspiration behind his new wedding collection?"

"No comment," she replied.

"Are you engaged?" another reporter called out.

Jansen sighed and sped up.

"Will you two get married in Paris during Fashion Week?"

She ducked inside Starbucks and crossed over to the bathroom. Pulling out her phone, she called Donovan to see if his day had been as crazy as hers. "Hello?"

"Donovan," she said. "Please tell me you aren't getting bombarded with calls?"

"Since about six this morning. Try explaining all those calls to my assistant, who has *Hot News* as her home page, that we are not dating."

"Oh, wow."

"I thought the blogs would run the picture, but this coverage is ridiculous."

"I guess your wedding line has everyone thinking you have matrimony on the brain."

"Whatever. Matrimony money. It's amazing how much a woman will pay for a dress she's only going to wear once."

"Careful, you're starting to sound jaded."

"You're not recording this, are you?" Donovan laughed. "I don't think you'd want to sell our conversation, since I'm making you the star of my line. Besides, you're not some groupie with nothing to lose."

"You're horrible, you know that."

"Anyway," he said, "how are you going to address this? Me, I'll just ignore it. But if you want to release a joint statement, I'm with it."

"I don't know what to do, but I'm already over the media chasing me. All I wanted to do was meet my assistant for lunch."

"You know, I'm all for toying with the media. Free publicity for my upcoming line, but if your man—"

"That's a problem I don't have." Instantly, she thought of Bradley. Had he seen any of this? Did he care? Or was he having a good laugh with his new boo?

"And why is that? You're rich, beautiful and smart. And you're single, I don't get it."

She had a two-word answer on the tip of her tongue. Bradley Stephens. He'd been the one man she had ever allowed to get into her mind and soul. And after all she gave him, she'd been left with a broken heart. The pain from her breakup with Bradley had taught her one valuable lesson—never fall in love again.

"I'm good with focusing on my career right now," she replied. "We can deal with this after Paris. I'm worn-out already."

"Where are you and your assistant meeting for lunch?"

"At db Bistro."

"Why don't I join you and add more fuel to the fire and show you how to confuse the rumor mill."

"I'm sure Dove would love for you to join us."

"Your assistant's name is Dove?"

"Yes," Jansen said with a laugh. "And no bird jokes."

"I make no promises. I'll see you guys in a little bit."

Jansen walked out of the bathroom happy to see that the media hounds had moved on. She was sure the Starbucks baristas had had a hand in their disappearance, so she dropped a few bills in the tip jar then headed for the bistro.

Chapter 4

Bradley shook his head and tried to pretend he wasn't affected when Kenyon showed him the picture of Jansen and some designer on his tablet. "Good for her," he said then gulped his water.

"You're a terrible liar. If you could see your face."

"It's been damn near three years. What was I supposed to expect?"

"I know you wanted her to come back to Atlanta and be by your side. And don't tell me that's not the case. Every *girlfriend* you had after her has been a clone of Jansen Douglas."

"There's no such thing as a clone of Jansen. She's one of a kind." With a far-off look in his eyes, Bradley picked up his glass of water. "She's going to be at Shelby's wedding."

"Probably with her man. Damn, you really messed that up. I bet Mama isn't happy about that decision."

Setting his glass down, Bradley chuckled. "You're right about that. She loved Jansen as much as I do."

Kenyon slammed his hand on the table. "I knew it! You've been pining away for that woman all of these years. Why didn't you just support the girl's ambitions?"

"Because I'm tired of losing people I love. I knew she was going to be one of the world's top models. She couldn't do that in Atlanta. And," he said, pointing to the iPad, "she needed to find someone who understands that world. It looks like she did."

"That's bullshit. If you love her, you should let her know that. I don't see a wedding band yet."

"Whoa, whoa, who are you and what have you done with my cynical big brother?"

"Life's too short to be lonely," Kenyon said as he cut into his waffle. "If there's a shot for you and Jansen, why not find out?"

"Because she's about to marry someone else?"

Kenyon shrugged. "Until she says *I do*, you have a chance."

I blew my chances a long time ago, he thought as he cut into his omelet.

After eating, the brothers headed to their parents' burial site. It was a cool Atlanta morning and on the anniversary of losing Joan and Winston, they all needed time to reflect. As soon as Bradley and Kenyon walked up to the mausoleum, Bradley's cell phone rang. And as he expected, it was Shelby.

"What's up, little sister," he said.

"I—I woke up and looked at the calendar and I've been crying all day," she said.

"I'm going to put you on speaker. Kenyon and I are at—"

"I wish I was there, too," she said. "Ken, hi."

"Hey, little princess," he replied.

"I haven't been called that in a while. You guys went to the West Egg Café this morning, didn't you?"

"Sure did," Bradley said.

"I always wondered why you two and Daddy loved that place so much."

"Same reason that you and Mama loved Macy's," Kenyon said.

Shelby's laughter made them smile. "We just needed some girl time. Lord knows, Sunday was all about football with the three of you."

"Does your fiancé like football?" Bradley asked.

"Not really."

"That's not good," Bradley said.

"Why haven't we met him?" Kenyon inquired.

"So, y'all are just going to team up on me? Today of all days?" Shelby whined. "Have either of you come to Paris to visit us?"

"Like we have time for that," the brothers said in concert.

"You could make time," she said.

Kenyon and Bradley looked at each other and shook their heads. "Fine," Bradley said. "We'll be there next week."

"And stay until the wedding?" The hope in her voice meant they would be in Paris for the next two weeks.

"Hey, Shell," Kenyon said. "Did you invite Jansen to your wedding?"

"Kenyon!" Bradley exclaimed. "Ignore him, Shelby."

"Actually, I did. She's going to be in Paris for Fashion Week anyway, so the timing was perfect."

"You still talk to Jansen?" Bradley asked despite himself.

"All the time. Wait, I'm not supposed to tell you this.

Our rule is, I don't talk about you and I don't funnel information to you."

"The gossip site mentioned Jansen's fiancé. Have you met him?" Bradley asked, ignoring the last part of her statement.

"No, and I'm kind of surprised. She never... Bradley, I'm not having this conversation with you. I don't know what you did to Jansen, but I'm not about to get into the middle of it."

"Girl," Kenyon said. "Spill it."

"No."

"Then I'm going to stop payment on that check to that wedding planner, who is charging way too much anyway," Kenyon said, while holding back his laughter.

Shelby started speaking broken French, telling her oldest brother that he was a vat of chicken fat and should be tossed in the ocean.

"Do you even know what you just said?" Bradley asked.

"It doesn't matter, I'm not going to sit up here and tell you her personal business when you broke her heart."

"Bye, Shelby," he said. After hanging up with his sister, Kenyon turned to Bradley and shook his head.

"You know she's right."

"You started this," Bradley exclaimed. A brisk wind blew over them.

"Either Mama or Daddy sent that," Kenyon said. "You better calm down and figure out how you're going to get the one woman who you ever loved to be yours again."

Bradley dropped his head. "That's going to be easier said than done. Shelby's right, I broke her heart and acted like a selfish jackass." Another breeze hit them. "Sorry for the language, Ma."

Kenyon laughed and wrapped his arm around his brother's slumping shoulders. "Come on, we have to plan a trip to Paris."

Jansen picked at her food while Dove stared at Donovan as if he was a living and breathing Egyptian god. Of course, he loved the adulation. Jansen hid her laughter as Dove reached out to wipe a smidge of sauce from Donovan's cheek with her napkin.

"You don't want to be caught on camera with a face full of marinara sauce," she said, then dropped her hand.

"Thank you, Bird of Beauty," he replied. "But I'm hoping we can avoid cameras for the rest of the day." Donovan pulled out his tablet and opened the Procreate app. "This is what I'm thinking about for the showstopper."

Dove looked over his shoulder. "Wow."

Jansen was speechless as she looked at the pink-and-ivory lace dress. The mermaid dress looked as if it was going to be curve hugging, and the bodice was just amazing. A low-cut neckline, lace and beading intricately weaved together. "Wow," Jansen said. "This is amazing."

"Just a first draft. I want to play around with the hemline. Maybe the mermaid thing is played. What are women trying to look like on their wedding day anyway?"

"Beautiful," Dove said. "She wants to be the only woman her groom has eyes for and she wants him to be eager to take that dress off her."

Donovan smiled. "You've really thought about this, huh?"

"What woman doesn't have those thoughts?"

Jansen silently said that she didn't, at least not anymore. But she knew the dress Donovan was working on would do everything Dove said, and more. "I don't think you need to change a thing about this dress," Jansen said.

Donovan nodded. "I thought you'd say that. When I drew this, I thought about you the whole time."

"It does look like something you'd wear," Dove said.

"I think—" Jansen's phone rang, interrupting her. Looking down at the screen, she saw it was Shelby. "I have to take this." She rose to her feet and headed into an empty corner. "Hey, Shelby."

"*Bonjour.* You know, I'm trying really hard not to be pissed off with you," she said.

"What are you talking about?"

"You and Donovan Strange."

"Oh. My. God. That news has gone international already?"

"So, it's true? Bradley will be so heartbroken."

"It's not true and why would your brother care?"

Shelby cleared her throat. "We're still doing this no talking about Bradley, right?"

Jansen narrowed her eyes, though her friend couldn't see her. "What did you do, Shelby Elaine?"

"Whoa, you went full government name. I didn't do anything. I just told him that I didn't know about your fiancé."

"I'm not engaged," Jansen said.

"So, you two are just dating?"

"We're not even— Again, why would Bradley care? I'm sure his woman is doing everything he needs her to do and he doesn't have to worry about her stepping out of line and wanting to follow her own path."

"Jansen, I've never asked because I was following

the rules, but I have to know—do you still love my brother?"

"I have to go."

"That means yes! Jansen, maybe you two need to talk. See if there is a second chance for—"

"I don't want to talk about Bradley, especially not today. By the way, how are you?"

"I'm feeling a lot better because I had a conversation with my brothers."

Jansen smiled despite herself. "I'm glad you had a chance to talk to them. How's Kenyon?" she asked, knowing that he and his mother had been at odds before her death.

"Kenyon and Bradley are fine. I tried to guilt them into coming to Paris. Not sure if it worked or not. But they want to meet Jacques and we're not going to Atlanta."

Atlanta. Jansen hadn't been back to that city since she and Bradley broke up. Three years ago, she'd even turned down a job in the Georgia Peach Fashion Show. It would've been a hundred-thousand-dollar payday, but no amount of money would allow her to return to Atlanta.

The last thing she'd ever wanted had been to run in to Bradley and his wife. In her mind, she'd built up a future for her ex and she didn't want to see it firsthand. She hadn't been ready to see another woman living the life that she *still* dreamed about. As much as she'd wanted to hate Bradley, she couldn't. But she wasn't about to pull the bandage off that wound.

"I'm glad you're okay today and don't believe everything you read on the internet."

"So, you're not getting married? I mean, Donovan Strange is a good-looking man and I wouldn't..."

"Business associates. That's all. I've had my one shot at love, it missed the mark and I'm good with that," she said.

"Do you believe in second chances?"

"Bye, Shelby."

"Wait, wait…"

"Seriously, I have to go. There are a dozen photographers snapping my picture through the window. Who knows what stories they're going to make up now."

"All right. Call me later."

Jansen sighed when she hung up, hating to lie to her friend, but she wasn't going to be drawn into a conversation about Bradley. Why was Shelby trying to change the rules of their friendship all of a sudden? Wait a minute! Had Bradley seen the pictures of her and Donovan? Ha! *I know good and well that he isn't pretending that he gives a damn.* Walking back to the table, Jansen forced herself to join in the conversation with Dove and Donovan. It didn't take long for her to get caught up in Donovan's designs and pick out a few dresses that she wanted to wear immediately.

"I'm going to make sure I send you and Dove some samples before heading to Paris," he said, then turned to Dove. "What are you? Size eight?"

"Oh my goodness, you guessed that by just looking at me?" she asked, her eyes sparkling.

"It's my job to know all the intricate details of a beautiful woman's body."

Jansen shook her head as she watched her assistant fall hook, line and sinker for Donovan's corny line.

"You do a great job of it," Dove replied with her hands underneath her chin.

"Have you ever thought about modeling?" he asked.

Dove shook her head. "No, not at all," she said,

then nodded toward Jansen. "I want to work behind the scenes. Jansen said there's more money in ownership than just being another pretty face in the crowd."

Donovan smiled. "She's right."

"I want to be an agent," Dove said. Jansen swelled with pride. Her assistant would be a great agent.

"That's right," Jansen said. "Dove is going to be one of the first women I take under my wing to teach about this industry."

"Are you coming to Paris with us?" he asked.

Dove shrugged. "I thought you were just going to Paris for your friend's wedding."

"It is Fashion Week and Donovan made me an offer I can't refuse."

Donovan grinned. "I really hope you mean that," he said, then he reached into his saddlebag and pulled out two plane tickets. "We're leaving tomorrow."

"What?" Jansen asked, furrowing her brow. "Donovan, that's a little—"

"Listen," he said. "Paris is beautiful this time of year and I want to get the best lace and materials to make this collection unlike any other that I've ever done. All of these designs are tailored to fit you, Jansen. I need you."

She smiled. "I guess we're going to Paris, Dove."

Dove clapped her hands. "Oh my goodness! This is so exciting."

Donovan took Dove's left hand in his and kissed it. *"Vous n'avez encore rien vu."*

She shook her head. "I have no idea what you said, but okay."

"He said," Jansen began, "you ain't seen nothin' yet."

"Jansen, you know everything," Donovan said.

"I wouldn't say that, but French is my second language," she said with a wink.

Chapter 5

Paris, France

"They're kissing again," Kenyon whispered to Bradley as they looked at Shelby and Jacques, who were sitting across from them at Aux Folies, a bar that seemed like a blast from Paris's bohemian past. The drinks were great. The quiet atmosphere was supposed to allow Bradley and Kenyon to get to know their future brother-in-law. All they knew so far was that Shelby enjoyed sticking her tongue down his throat.

"Damn, y'all," Bradley said as he slapped the table. "Nobody wants to see this."

"Sorry," Jacques said. "But this place brings out the lover in—"

"Hey, dude, that's my little sister," Kenyon growled.

"Excuse me," Shelby said. "I'm a grown woman. *Je suis une femme adulte.*"

"Oui, tu l'es, ma chérie," Jacques replied, then kissed her hand. Bradley and Kenyon rolled their eyes. Though they could do without all of the PDAs, they liked Jacques. It seemed that his love had reformed Shelby's wild-child ways. Bradley couldn't help but notice his sister's higher necklines and lower hemlines. He was impressed. But still, he could go his whole life without watching her share intimate kisses in public with this man.

"Anyway," Bradley said, "since you two are familiar with the inside of each other's mouths, are we going to get to know our future brother-in-law?"

Shelby shrugged. "You know, there's a big fashion show at the Belle Époque. And I'm not saying Jansen's going to be there. But she might be."

Bradley rolled his eyes. "Really?"

"I'm sick of both of you. Why do you think y'all are in Paris at the same time?"

"Because you invited her to your wedding. She's here with her man," Bradley said, remembering the cover of a French tabloid that he'd seen at breakfast.

"That's not—"

"I'm not going to a fashion show, all right," Kenyon said. "Let's find a football game or something. I have no interest in sitting around watching—wait a minute. Is it a lingerie show?"

Shelby tossed her napkin at her older brother. "Perv!"

"Whatever. The after parties are what make going to these shows exciting," she said.

"Aw, the party girl is still in there, huh?" Bradley said and shook his head.

Shelby tossed her head. "I'm not as old as you are, I can still have a good time. If we don't go to the show, then we have to go to Benoît Mason's after party. He's raising money for Senegal girls and the school Dawn Marie Senghor plans to open. It's a party with a purpose," she said, then stuck her tongue out at him.

"And what purpose would that be? Meddling in my life?" he mumbled.

"Everything isn't about you, Bradley Stephens!" She turned to her fiancé. "See what I've been telling you," she said in French.

"And just what have you been telling him?" Bradley asked with a laugh.

"Nothing more than that you two are very protective of her," Jacques replied.

"Yeah, right," Kenyon said with a snort. "Listen, Jack. We love our sister and I think you love her, too. If you guys are going to have a life in Paris, we have to know that you have her best interests at heart."

Jacques nodded. "I do," he said, taking Shelby's hand into his. "I've never known a more beautiful and loving woman. I'm just glad she said yes when I asked her to be my wife. My life will be about making her happy and keeping her safe."

"And making babies. Let's not forget about the babies," Shelby said with a smile.

"TMI," Bradley said, then broke into laughter. Inside, he was wondering how many kids he and Jansen would have welcomed into the world if he hadn't allowed her to walk out of his life. Downing his drink, Bradley actually hoped he wouldn't see Jansen with her new man. He wasn't ready to handle that.

Jansen shook her head as she watched Dove talking to the makeup artist who would be applying the peacock lashes Jansen would be wearing in the show. How did she allow herself to get talked into working?

She was supposed to be enjoying a vacation in Paris. Hanging out with her friend before she got married. *Donovan Strange!*

"It'll build a buzz for our big show," he'd said as he told her about the opening in the inaugural April in Paris Fashion Week.

"You make me sick," she'd replied before agreeing. After all, she loved the runway.

Now, here she was about to do a show knowing that Bradley could be in the audience. When she'd called Shelby after landing at Charles de Gaulle Airport, her friend dropped the bomb on her.

Bradley's in Paris. And, of course, she'd come to the show. Jansen knew she'd bring her brother in the name of showing him around the city. And just because Shelby hadn't mentioned a wife didn't mean one didn't exist. Knowing Shelby, she probably didn't like her and wanted Jansen to drive a wedge between the couple.

"Not falling for it," she mumbled as the makeup artist and Dove walked over to her.

"Talking to yourself is never a good sign," Dove said, glancing at the outfit Jansen would be wearing as the showstopper. "This is going to be a fierce show! I love the feathers, and with your legs, girl, you're going be all over the fashion trades."

Jansen studied the blue, gold and green bodysuit with the peacock feathers decorating the bodice. It screamed Beyoncé. Jansen loved how it had hugged her body at the fitting. Though she wasn't happy about the lashes that would accompany the outfit, she knew it would photograph well. When the makeup artist started working on her face, Jansen pushed all thoughts of Bradley and everything else out of her head. It was showtime and she was about to give good face.

An hour later, Jansen almost didn't recognize herself and gave the makeup artist high praise and a high five. The lashes she'd been so worried about looked amazing on her eyes, complemented by the blue-and-purple eye shadow. Her lips were painted a matted gold color and the foundation blended in with her skin, making her look flawless.

"You look like a goddess," Dove said as the hairstylist fluffed the curly wig she'd finished fitting to Jansen's head.

"That's the goal, luv," the hairstylist said. "Jansen, thank you for letting me debut my new wig on you. This is going to be so epic."

"Thank you for thinking that my big head would look this amazing underneath this wig. I know I'll be getting a few," she said as she touched the Foxy Brown-esque wig.

"I hope one will be for me," Dove said with a smile. "You know I love this."

Winking at her assistant, she started to tell her that all of the wigs would be hers. On her days off, Jansen wasn't one for getting glammed up. She'd pull her hair into a ponytail or a bun, maybe put on some lip gloss and head out unbothered. Well, until this rumor with Donovan started. So far, the press in Paris had been kind. Then again, Donovan had been so busy promoting his line that he and Jansen hadn't been seen together since they got off the plane.

After getting dressed, Jansen waited in the wings for her cue. She loved runway work, but tonight, she was nervous; even more nervous than she'd been walking in her first professional show. What if he was really out there? *Don't do this to yourself,* she thought as the music changed and the producer gave her the signal to head out to the stage. She put her game face on, ignoring the audience and strutting across the runway as Daft Punk's "Get Lucky" blared through the speakers. She shimmied a bit as she got to the end of the runway, eliciting a roar from the crowd. Turning her head to the side, Jansen did what the industry knew her for, she gave face: a half smile, eyes sparkling and a bit of a lip quiver. And just as she turned her head to the other side, that's when she saw a heart-aching blast from the past watching her every move. Bradley. She blinked. She nearly stumbled but recovered quickly. Jansen raised the edge of her lip, then turned and made another pass on the runway as Beyoncé's "Flawless" began playing. Putting a little extra in her strut, Jansen had never been so happy to get offstage. Her heart pounded like the bass from the music as she realized she was going to have to hit the stage again with the designer.

I just won't look in his direction. Maybe that wasn't even Bradley, she thought as the curtain opened for the models to take their final walk.

Bradley sat in stunned silence. Jansen Douglas was even more beautiful and curvaceous than he remembered. And those legs. Damn it, he wanted to hop on that stage and wrap them around his waist and never let her go. Kenyon kept shaking his head, telling Bradley that he'd messed up.

"One more time," he snapped at his brother, "and I'm going to knock you back to Atlanta."

"Shh!" Shelby said.

"Her husband is going to be a lucky man," Kenyon jabbed one more time. "And to think, she used to love you."

Bradley stood up and the music started again. Shelby

tugged at his pant leg and told him to sit down. He stared at the stage as Jansen walked out with a short blonde woman who he assumed designed that wonderful outfit that his woman wore. Wait. *His woman?* Was he insane? It was all over the tabloids that Jansen was engaged. But seeing her on the runway brought back the beautiful memories, wanton thoughts and the heartbreaking mistake that he had made. And again, he regretted allowing his selfish need to keep her close to him ruin the best thing that had ever happened to him. Now she was someone else's. But what if Shelby was right and it wasn't too late to fix things? And wait, did she just look at him and frown?

"I guess she's not happy to see you," Shelby whispered. "Jansen never does that."

"Shut up."

"I still believe you two should talk. I'm going to go backstage and say hi. You should come with me."

Bradley was about to remind his sister that Jansen had a man, until he looked up on the stage and saw her walking away. Her round bottom made his body twitch. "Okay," he said. "Let's go."

"Wait for me," Kenyon said with a laugh. The icy glare Bradley shot him alerted Kenyon that his joke wasn't appreciated. As Bradley followed Shelby backstage, he felt a chill run down his spine. He hadn't seen Jansen in forever and now he was about to be inches from her. About to see her in her element, living her dream—with another man.

Jansen wiped her face with an oatmeal makeup-remover pad and covered her shoulders with a plush white towel. Twice, she'd looked at Bradley and allowed her emotions to get the best of her onstage. That wasn't what she did. She was the Face. How had she allowed this man to get inside her head like that? Kicking her heels off and reaching for a short robe, she heard him.

"Hello, Jansen."

Whirling around, standing there in a thong and nothing else, she locked eyes with Bradley.

"What are you doing here?" she asked, not bothering to cover her nudity. And as much as he tried to meet her sparkling eyes, Bradley couldn't look past her round brown breasts, remembering taking those diamond-hard nipples into his mouth and making her moan in delight. She followed his eyes and crossed her arms across her chest.

"You look amazing. I mean, looked amazing onstage."

"That's what you have to say to me after all these years?" she asked as she turned her back to him and put her robe on. "Shelby, I'm going to shoot you."

"I tried to stop him from coming back here," she fibbed. Bradley shot his sister a quizzical look.

"I'm sure you did," Jansen said. "Nice to see you both, but I have to get out of here."

Bradley reached out and touched Jansen's elbow as she brushed past him. She jerked away as if his hand was a flame. "Jansen," he whispered. "It's good seeing you and I'd like to talk to you before—"

Donovan and Dove burst backstage, both holding several bouquets of roses. "You were amazing!" Donovan said. "I can't wait to see you in my wedding dress."

Bradley felt his heart drop to his feet. He didn't even stick around to see her man embrace her.

Shelby, noting her brother's crestfallen face, followed him out of the backstage area.

"Are you okay?"

"Thanks for throwing me under the bus and making

me look like a damn fool. Thought you said she wasn't getting married?"

"That's what she told me."

"He clearly said he couldn't wait to see her in a wedding dress. I don't think there's any doubt about her relationship status. Why did I let you talk me into coming to this show and especially coming back here?"

"I swear, when I talked to her last week, she said don't believe everything you read, I assumed—"

"Shelby, don't worry about it. Let's get out of here, I need a drink." Bradley walked away from his sister shaking his head.

"Maybe you can talk to Jansen at the party."

Bradley stopped in his tracks. "Why would I want to talk to Jansen? She's probably going to be hugged up, sipping champagne with her man who can't wait to see her in a wedding dress. I'm going back to the hotel." He stormed off and Shelby headed backstage to find Jansen.

"Hey, pretty lady, what's with the scowl?" Donovan asked Jansen as she harshly combed her hair.

"Nothing. Tired, I guess."

Dove shook her head. "Was that who I think it was with your girl Shelby?" She wiggled her eyebrows and Jansen almost had a hysterical-supermodel moment, but there wasn't a cell phone in sight.

"Dove, I'm not talking about that man."

"Uh-oh," Donovan said. "Sounds like I need to leave you two alone for some girl talk."

"No," Jansen said, standing up and fully dressed in a gold minidress and sky-high purple heels. "I'm in Paris to have a good time and celebrate my friend's wedding."

"And model my dress and announce the Jansen Proj-

ect. You have a lot to do here in gay Paree," he said
with an exaggerated accent. "Dove and I can't have
all the fun."

Jansen shrugged and glanced at the roses she'd received. Knowing that many of her supporters and people she'd need to help her with her business venture
would be at the after party, she had to focus on the future. But how could she when her mind was stuck in
the past?

Chapter 6

Sitting in his hotel room, Bradley wondered if he should go to the after party to get his punishment for being dumb enough to allow Jansen to walk out of his life. Maybe he needed to see her with her new man to make sure she was happy.

She deserved to be happy. Rising to his feet, he paced back and forth filled with regret and jealousy. Did that clown who wanted to see her in his wedding dress know that Jansen hated thunderstorms? Did he know that she wasn't a fan of milk chocolate and preferred dark chocolate with almonds? Did he know that when she was stressed out, a foot massage calmed her down instantly?

"Shit," he muttered. "I can't lose her again."

Stepping into his Italian loafers, Bradley decided that he would go to the after party and this time, he would talk to Jansen. Fiancé or not. When he made it to the lobby, he wasn't upset to see his sister and Jacques leaving without notifying him. In fact, he hoped that everyone thought he was upstairs moping. He needed a one-on-one with Jansen and the less his siblings knew about his plan the better.

The party was about three blocks away from the hotel, which made Bradley happy since he'd decided to walk. Arriving at the location, he wasn't at all surprised to see that he was woefully underdressed—in a pair of dark jeans and a button-down white shirt. Part of him thought about the money that was being spent on this party and how it could save so many lives. *Just a waste,* he thought bitterly. Sighing, Bradley decided that he wasn't going to storm in there when he knew that—

"Bradley?" Jansen called out. Turning around, he watched as she sauntered his way. And boy, was she wearing that skintight gold dress.

"Yes," he said, his eyes appreciatively roaming her body. "I was…uh, just leaving."

"Funny, looked like you'd just gotten here."

"Honestly, I had. I was looking for you," he said.

"Why?"

"Because it's been a long time and I need to tell you something."

She placed her hand on her hip and raised her perfectly manicured right eyebrow. "Well?"

"I think we could at least sit down over a cup of coffee or breakfast and talk like civilized people."

She blinked and Bradley half expected her to walk away. "That's fine and you're right, we should talk. I'd love to ease this awkwardness between us so that we can all enjoy Shelby's upcoming wedding."

Bradley smiled. "And…" Before he could finish, Donovan called Jansen's name. *Damn,* he thought as he watched the man jog toward her. It was the same guy from backstage. Her fiancé.

"Donovan, I thought I was late. Where's Dove?" she asked.

"She hooked up with a few of her friends at Bar La Vue." Donovan looked from Jansen to Bradley. "Am I interrupting something here?"

"No, just catching up with an old f— This is Shelby's brother," she said. Bradley felt Jansen's introduction was a little weird. *Shelby's brother? That's how you feel, or is your man that jealous?* Donovan extended his hand to Bradley.

"Nice to meet you," he said. Bradley barely shook his hand, wondering if that was the same hand he used to hold and touch Jansen in the most intimate places. Places that he used to frequent, places that he discovered.

"Jansen, I'm staying at—"

"I know where you're staying," she said. "Shelby told me when she called and apologized for what happened after the fashion show."

Donovan raised his eyebrow but didn't say anything. Bradley was not impressed with this man. What was he? Jansen's lapdog? He'd be damned if he would've let that go without some sort of question.

"I guess I'll see you at Shelby's brunch."

Jansen furrowed her brows, then she smiled. She'd almost forgotten about tomorrow's festivities. She'd also noticed the cold looks he gave Donovan, making it obvious that he'd read the blogs and heard the rumors about her so-called engagement. Jansen wondered where his wife was, because she refused to believe that he was still single in Atlanta. Then again, he was probably having a great time playing the field. Why wouldn't he?

From what she understood, Atlanta was a player's paradise these days, and as much as she hated to admit it, Bradley had gotten better with time. His ebony-brown skin was just as smooth as it had always been, those eyes, whiskey brown and bright. She looked down at his hands, the hands that had tenderly taught her about passion, touched her in the most intimate places.

Jansen shivered inwardly as she thought about his long fingers splitting her wet folds of flesh and stroking her precious pearl. The first time he'd touched her there, she'd come. Had a feeling of heat that she'd never felt before in her life, and over the years, he'd given her those feelings again and again.

Stop it, she admonished herself as she watched his lips move. Those lips were even more magical than his hands.

"Jansen?" Donovan asked.

"What?" she replied, blinking at him, realizing that she was not in Atlanta but on a sidewalk in Paris. Still, Bradley was there. And he was alone.

"You want to go in?" he asked. She looked at Bradley, who had given her a two-finger salute and started to walk away. But she had questions and she was about to call his name, but the words died on her tongue. She watched him walk away and then turned back to Donovan. Her smile was intact. "Let's go," she said.

"I'm not even going to ask what that was all about."

"Good, because I don't want to talk about it."

Donovan shrugged and they walked into the party, but Jansen was hardly on her A-game after seeing Bradley Stephens.

Bradley wandered into a small coffee shop to catch his breath. He knew Jansen wasn't in love with that guy.

And he wondered if that man had an idea as to what he meant to Jansen. *Game on,* Bradley decided as he walked up to the counter and ordered a cup of coffee in broken French.

When he got his café au lait, Bradley headed outside and sat at a table near the sidewalk. Paris was beautiful at night, and he closed his eyes for a moment, dreaming that he and Jansen were celebrating their fifth or sixth wedding anniversary. Maybe they would've been here with their children—a little girl with eyes like her mom's.

"Bradley?"

Opening his eyes, he saw Jansen standing there. Was he still dreaming? Nope, because there she was in that gold dress.

"I thought you were going to that party back there," he said, keeping his voice cool. Then he nodded toward the empty seat at his table.

Jansen paused for a moment, then she sat down. Bradley wanted to smile, wanted to launch into an apology, but she had another man and probably didn't care what he had to say. Wait a minute. Why was her man allowing her to walk around the streets of Paris by herself? This was a foreign city and who knew what the crime rate was. "Why are you out here alone?"

"It was a little too crowded and I needed some air. I must say, seeing you threw me for a loop."

"Really?"

She rolled her eyes. "Bradley, we have history. There was a time when I thought we would be together forever, but…"

"I messed that up. I guess you're going to get your happily ever after with that guy. Congratulations, Jansen. But how does he feel knowing you ditched him to find me?"

"I didn't come to find you. I see you still think the sun doesn't rise until it hits your ass. You haven't changed at all, have you?"

"Oh, I've changed. And so have you."

"What's that supposed to mean?"

"You're even more beautiful than I remember."

A heated blush filled her cheeks, crept down her neck and finally settled between her thighs. "It's the makeup and…"

"No, Jansen, it's you. You've always been gorgeous. Maybe I wasn't ready to share you with the world. I should've been more supportive of what you wanted rather than thinking you should have hidden your light."

She shot him a blank look. "You wanted everything your way, how did that work out for you?"

"I should probably thank you," he said.

"Thank me?"

He nodded and took a sip of his drink, trying and failing not to look at her cleavage. "I realized that day that I can't expect my woman to do everything I want her to. And though I thought the center meant as much to you as it did to me, I shouldn't have made that assumption for you. I still believe with your brain you could've done something more with your life. You could've been on the front line teaching these young girls the value of their lives."

She wondered if he even realized how saying that three years ago would've changed their lives. But right now he sounded like a pompous jerk. Jansen narrowed her eyes at him. "A little too late," she said.

"Better late than never. I'm also thankful for your generosity," he said. "The donations that you make every year help us further our cause of helping families and victims of domestic violence."

"I loved your parents and what they stood for. I'm glad that I can help their legacy continue."

"You could've done a lot more if you stayed on staff…"

"You're really going to start that again?"

"No," he said as he eased closer to her chair. "I'm going to start this." He cupped her face in his hands and kissed her slowly, deliberately and passionately. He slipped his hands between her thighs and a soft moan escaped her throat. Jansen trembled with anticipation, with longing. Inside, Bradley beamed, knowing she still belonged to him. Still clamored for his touch as much as he yearned for her.

Breaking the kiss, he looked into Jansen's eyes.

"Do you love him?"

"What?" she asked, blinking rapidly.

"Well, do you?"

"Are you serious? You're jealous of tabloid headlines?"

"No, I'm just wondering what kind of man allows the woman he's supposed to marry to walk the streets of Paris alone. If you were my woman, I would never allow that to happen."

Jansen rose to her feet and glared at him. "Yeah, you're the same as you've always been. Still want to be in control of everything. All men don't think like you, thank God. Why don't we just call it a life? There's nothing else we need to say to one another."

Bradley stood up and closed the space between them. "There's plenty to say," he said. "I've never stopped loving you and—" He stroked her arm. "I can feel how much you want me, Jansen. So, forgive me if I don't celebrate your engagement. And I'm not going to watch you marry a man that you may like but don't love."

"I am—" Bradley silenced her with a kiss that made her knees quiver. His tongue filled her mouth, reminding her that no one could kiss like Bradley, no one could find the way to her soul with a kiss. No one but Bradley. And when he pulled her against his hard body, she felt the throbbing of all his muscles and melted against him. She wanted to peel her dress off and let him have his way with her. She wanted to go back to the days when she and Bradley woke up entwined in each other's arms and the previous night's passion became that morning's desire.

His hand slipped between her thighs again, wanting to touch her in the most intimate way. Jansen knew this had to stop. Pulling back from him, she pushed him away and shook her head. Without another word, she took off down the street.

Jansen didn't want to go back to the party, she didn't want to be around people right now. What she wanted to do was go back to that café and kiss Bradley again. She'd dreamed of that kiss for years. Dreamed of a happy reunion with him, had the nightmare of believing he was married to some docile woman who did everything he wanted. *If that's the case, why did he kiss you and tell you that he still loves you?* her inner voice questioned. She stopped and turned around, Jansen had every intention of heading back to the café. She gasped when she saw Bradley approaching her.

"I don't believe you should be wandering around the streets dressed like that. Paris or not," he said.

"Why did you kiss me?"

"Because I needed to."

"Bradley, we're over. I've moved on and I'm sure

you have, too. Don't let the mythology of Paris make you think that—"

"Paris, New York or Atlanta, what I said doesn't change."

"Really?" She shook her head and sighed deeply. "What changed, Bradley? Because, as I recall, love to you meant doing everything your way."

"Think about where I was when you came to me. My parents had just died and I was trying to hold on to everything too tight."

She snorted and shook her head. "Everything that you just said would've made a hell of a difference back then."

"Time and distance. But I guess I'm too late, since you have moved on."

"You're right, it's too late and there is no need to go rewriting history and pretending there's a future between us."

Bradley stroked her cheek. "You never answered my question."

She wanted to succumb to the tingles his touch sent rushing though her body. "I—I don't have to," Jansen said, then snatched away from him. "I'm going to my hotel. Alone." Bradley grabbed her arm.

"So, you're willing to settle for safe? Willing to have a life without love because—"

"You broke my heart!" she shouted. "You broke my damn heart and I'm not going to let that happen again. Now, take your hand off me!"

He let her go but didn't let her continue to walk alone. They walked in silence for two blocks. "Why are you following me?" she snapped when they ended up in front of her hotel. "Because I'm not inviting you up."

"I didn't ask you to. I just wanted to make sure you

made it here safely. Get some rest. I'll see you tomorrow."

"That's not a good idea."

"I thought we needed to talk."

"I've said all I need to say."

"But I haven't, and since you're not inviting me in, we're going to have to finish this tomorrow."

"Shelby's brunch won't be the time or place."

"Then let's make right now the time and place."

Jansen looked toward the hotel entrance. She wanted to take him up to her room, wanted to kiss him, make love to him and remember why she'd fallen in love with him all those years ago. But she had to walk away. When Bradley reached out and stroked her cheek, her lips trembled.

"Jansen," he said, his voice a low groan. She tilted her head, and her lips crashed into his. The kiss was sweet, tender and demanding.

"Mmm," she moaned. "Bradley."

"Yes?"

"You still can't come up." With all the strength she could muster, Jansen walked inside.

Alone in the elevator, she leaned against the wall and prayed for the quivering in her knees to stop. She had to get her hormones under control before Shelby's brunch. But tonight, she was going to bask in the dreams of what would've happened had she invited Bradley in.

Chapter 7

The next morning, Bradley was up right at the crack of dawn. It wasn't as if he'd been able to sleep anyway. Jansen haunted his dreams like a sexy specter. As he looked over the city from his room, he wondered if she had spent the night wrapped in her fiancé's arms but thinking about him.

"Our story isn't over," he whispered as he watched the sunrise over the Seine. He wondered how he was going to keep his focus at this brunch. What if Jansen walked in with her fiancé? Something was off about that relationship. Turning away from the window, he headed for the bathroom to shower and prepare his seduction overture. Jansen wouldn't stand a chance when he was done.

"Bradley," Jansen moaned, then woke up—bolting upright in her bed. The cold and empty sheets reminded her that she'd only been making love to him in her dreams. Was she disappointed? Yes. The wetness between her thighs was another reminder of how much she wanted him. She pounded her pillow.

"Why am I torturing myself?" she groaned before flipping over on her face. It was just a few minutes after six and she couldn't go back to sleep for the life of her. She had to pull herself together to get ready for Shelby's brunch and seeing Bradley again. How was she going to face him after the wanton dreams she'd had about him? They were supposed to be easing the tension between them, not creating enough sexual heat that would cause the great Paris fire of the twenty-first century.

Maybe I should just go for a run, Jansen thought. After dressing in her running gear, she headed downstairs. When she spotted Donovan and Dove easing toward the elevators hand in hand, looking like reruns from last night, she couldn't help but smile.

Maybe the magic of Paris had wrapped its arms around those two, but she hoped that Dove wouldn't get her heart broken when they returned to New York. Then again, they were both adults and she had her own heart to worry about. Jansen ducked out the door without being seen by the duo. As she headed to the banks of the Seine, Jansen slowed her gait just to marvel at the sun rays reflecting off the river. The golden glow made her think of all the mornings that she and Bradley would wake up in his midtown Atlanta loft to the reflection of the state Capitol building bathing them in light. Naked. Wrapped in each other's arms. Jansen started running faster. The point of her morning jog was to stop thinking about having sex with Bradley, not to relive it.

After a three-mile run, Jansen was sweaty, tired and ravenous. Now she could go to the brunch and have a good time without thinking about ripping Bradley's clothes off. And she could finally take a nap!

Bradley was one of the first people to arrive at the brunch. Not because he was excited about eating, but because he wanted to be there the moment Jansen walked into the banquet room. He didn't give a damn if she was with her fiancé or not. He was going to whisk her off and show her the Jansen stone. Then he'd let her know that no one would love her the way he did.

The hotel crew began setting the tables and placing carafes of coffee in the center next to the calla lilies.

"Monsieur, êtes-vous bien?" a waiter asked.

"Oui," Bradley replied, then headed out into the hallway. So he was a little early. But he was determined to wait for Jansen. Pacing back and forth, he was wondering if he should have brought the Jansen stone to brunch. Yep, he needed to show her that ring, especially since he didn't see an engagement ring on her finger. What kind of man didn't put a ring on it to announce to the world that she was his?

"What's up, Bradley?" Kenyon said as he crossed over to his brother. "I figured you'd be here overseeing the festivities."

"Uh-huh."

"Jansen is probably going to make an entrance, so you could've slept in."

"Shut up," Bradley said. "And who said I'm waiting for Jansen?"

"Yeah, because you're concerned about the way the tables are going to look. Why don't you give this thing with Jansen a rest? Today is supposed to be about our little sister."

"Why don't you leave me alone?"

"Bradley, Jansen has moved on. Why don't you follow her lead?"

"Why don't you shut the hell up?" Bradley snapped. "I know what I'm doing."

"Man, you saw her fiancé. What you're doing is setting yourself up to get beat down."

Bradley was about to tell his brother how close he was to the same thing, when she walked in. He wanted nothing more than to kiss her again, peel that knee-skimming purple dress from her gorgeous body and make love to her.

"Kenyon," she said as she made her way over to the brothers.

"Hello, beautiful," he said, then gave her a tight hug. Bradley cleared his throat and gave Kenyon a sideways glance.

"Don't wrinkle her dress," Bradley said, thumping his brother on the shoulder. Letting Jansen go, Kenyon playfully smacked Bradley's shoulder.

"I see you two haven't changed," she said with a giggle. "Still fighting over everything. I'll never forget paper clip–gate."

Bradley shook his head at the memory and Kenyon groaned.

"I was trying to cut costs," Kenyon said.

"Three dollars," Jansen and Bradley said in concert.

"Forget both of y'all. I'm going inside."

When Kenyon walked away, Jansen looked up at Bradley and offered him a sheepish smile. "I guess we should go in, as well."

"You're not going to wait for your fiancé?"

She rolled her eyes. "Really?"

Bradley shrugged. "What kind of relationship do you and this—"

Jansen shook her head. "Do you believe everything you read?"

"What do you mean?"

"I'm not engaged."

"What?" Bradley didn't hide his smile at all. "I can't say I'm disappointed that the media got it wrong."

Placing her hand on her hip, Jansen tilted her head to the side. "Why does it matter what I do?"

He stroked her cheek. "I thought about you all night, couldn't wait for this moment right now," he replied.

Bradley's honesty startled her. Could she be that bold and tell him that she'd woken up with his name on her lips? Nope. Instead, she just smiled. "Well," she said. "Here we are."

"And you look stunning," he said. "Even better than in my dreams last night. But then again, you weren't wearing any panties last night in my fantasy."

"I'm here for brunch and to celebrate my friend's upcoming wedding. You can keep your dreams to yourself, all right?"

"I've done that for too long already. I'm laying my cards on the table, Jansen. I want you back."

She gasped and shook her head. "I'm going inside. This isn't the time or the place."

Bradley wrapped his arms around her waist and pulled her against his chest. She placed her hand on his chest and closed her eyes. It felt good being in his arms.

"We're not doing this. I know Paris is a city that makes everything feel so romantic, but I haven't heard from you for years. I'm not going to just—"

"And I've regretted that for a long time. I should've reached out to you and said that I was sorry."

"But you didn't seem to care about us until you

thought I was going to marry someone else. You only wanted what you thought you couldn't have."

"So, you're saying I can have you?"

Jansen wanted to swallow her words, wanted to tell him that he wasn't going to have anything. But she wanted him. Wanted to feel his lips against hers again.

"Let's be clear," Jansen began. "I'm not here to relive the past. I don't want to go back to the way things were."

"Neither do I. I need you in my future because I've already messed up our past."

"We're different people now," she said. "Maybe we just need closure."

"Closure?" he asked, raising his eyebrow.

Jansen nodded. "I'm going to be honest, I want you."

Bradley smiled. "I have a room upstairs. And just so we're clear, we aren't going upstairs to talk."

"Bradley," she whispered.

"Let's go upstairs."

"Wait," she said, placing her hand on his shoulder. "I should have at least said hello to Shelby…but for the record, I'm not wearing any panties."

Bradley nearly dropped to his knees when she said that. "Why are we still standing here?" He scooped her up in his arms and nearly sprinted to the elevator. Jansen wrapped her arms around his neck and inhaled his citrusy scent. That hadn't changed about him and she loved it. He smelled as good as she remembered— maybe even a little better. She brushed her lips against his neck. Bradley shivered and moaned. Those lips still knew how to command his body.

"You know if you keep doing that, we might not make it to my room."

She ran her tongue up and down his neck.

"Jansen," he intoned. "You're starting trouble."

"Then finish it," she replied saucily.

He stood Jansen against the mirrored wall of the elevator and pressed the emergency-stop button. Before she could ask him what he was doing, Bradley had dropped to his knees and had her dress around her waist. She wasn't wearing panties and he licked his lips before laying a slow kiss on her wet folds of flesh. His tongue teased her tenderness. Jansen moaned as his lips closed around her throbbing bud. Gripping the back of his head, she urged him to go deeper. Now using his tongue and index finger, Bradley had Jansen gushing like Old Faithful. Her moans turned to screams of passion as he lapped her sweet release.

She'd missed his touch, the way he made her body purr with excitement. No one else ever came close to making her feel as good and as satisfied as Bradley did. As he was doing as he lifted her left leg onto his shoulder and deepened his sensual kiss. Bracing herself against his shoulders, she gave in to the orgasm.

The elevator started moving again as Jansen collapsed on Bradley's shoulders. He picked her up and leaned against the wall. "Baby, you still taste so good," he said.

"Mmm," was the only reply she could muster.

"I guess Security figured out that there wasn't an emergency in here."

"Oh my God, I hope there's no video of what just happened," she said, placing her hand to her mouth.

"Let's pray TMZ doesn't have a Paris desk."

Jansen's eyes stretched to the size of quarters. "Don't say that. Oh my—"

He stroked her cheek. "Don't worry, baby, we're about to be behind closed doors," he said as the elevator came to a stop on his floor.

They rushed into his room. Bradley smoothly unlocked the door while stroking Jansen's bare behind underneath her dress. Jansen cooed as his hand split her thighs. Once he closed the door, Bradley pressed her against the wall and unzipped her dress. Slowly, he slid it down her shoulders, kissing her silky skin. With her breasts exposed, he stroked them gently, marveling at the softness of her chocolate orbs. Her erect nipples tingled and called out to his mouth. Bradley heeded the call and took the hard nubs into his mouth, altering between left and right, making Jansen call out his name. Her body shivered under the touch of his mouth. While he licked and sucked her supple breasts, his fingers probed her wetness, seeking and finding her throbbing bud. His fingers danced across that slick flesh until Jansen's desire poured from her like honey.

"That's it, baby," he whispered in her ear. "Come for me."

"Bradley," she cried. "I need you."

"I'm right here. You got me."

So many things ran through her mind, so many questions, and so many things that they should've said all of those years ago. Instead, she just called his name. Lifting her in his arms and letting the dress pool at her feet, Bradley carried her to the bed and drank in her naked image against the white satin sheets. Opening her arms, she called out his name and said something in French that made him hard as a brick.

When he joined her in the bed, Jansen kissed him slow and long as she unbuttoned his oxford shirt. Running her hands across his chest, she expelled a sigh. He was everything she'd remembered and more than she'd dreamed of last night. Part of her couldn't believe that they were here together. Pushing the shirt off his shoulders, she nibbled at his bottom lip. Bradley groaned as he took her hand and placed it on his zipper.

"Need. To. Be. Inside. You," he moaned. Jansen unzipped his slacks and stroked his erection. Bradley thought he was going to lose his mind as her hand moved back and forth, fast and slow. He pulled back from her, quickly stripped out of his clothes and shook his head at her.

"That was cruel," he said. Jansen straddled his body and smiled.

"And what would you called what you did to me in the elevator?" she asked then closed her lips around his neck while still working his most tender spot with her hand. Groaning, Bradley was pleasantly surprised by her aggressiveness and boldness when she snaked down his body and took his hardness into her mouth. He thought he was living in last night's fantasy.

Burying his hands in her hair, he let her control his pleasure, but as he felt the grips of his climax taking hold, he eased back from her, practically begging her to stop. "Let me get protection for us," he said.

She nodded. Bradley glanced over his shoulder at her as he walked to the closet and pulled a box of condoms from his suitcase.

"I guess you had big plans for Paris," she said when he approached the bed with the condoms.

"Would you rather I didn't have any?" he asked as he rejoined her in the bed. He slipped his hands between her thighs. "And then you'd be lying here wet and unsatisfied. We can't have that, now, can we."

"No," she moaned as his finger brushed against her hungry clitoris.

He smiled, recognizing the look of passion and need in her eyes. Bradley quickly sheathed his erection and pulled Jansen into his lap. "I want to look at you while you come," he whispered as he thrust into her awaiting valley. Jansen wrapped her arms around his neck and threw her head back as she matched him stroke for stroke. This was better than her wildest dreams. Looking into his eyes, she felt the heat, saw his desire and she was afraid.

Afraid because she had to admit that she still loved this man. "Bradley," she called out, then closed her eyes.

"Look at me, baby," he said. "Look at me."

She opened her eyes and blinked back her tears. Why did being with him have to feel so good?

"Love me," she moaned, tightening her thighs around his waist. He thrust forward, swimming in her wetness and wanting nothing more than to love her for the rest of his life.

Was this the beginning of their future? Could they start over and have the life that they should already be living? Bradley brought his lips down on top of hers and hoped that his kiss told her what he really wanted, her love as a staple in his life.

"Jansen, Jansen," he cried out after breaking their kiss. She closed her eyes, unable to face him knowing that this was going to be the last time that she could allow herself to feel like this.

When she reached her climax and collapsed against his chest, Jansen fought back the tears. Bradley stroked her back and kissed her cheek.

"You're still amazing," he breathed into her ear.

"Mmm, so are you."

"Jansen, I'm sorry."

She opened her eyes and blinked. "What?"

"I should've never allowed you to walk out of my office that day and led you to believe that I didn't care."

"It's a little too late to try to rewrite the past," she said. "What we just shared was magical and the closure that we need to move on."

He dropped his arms from around her. "What? Move on?" Bradley rose from the bed and crossed over to the closet. He pulled the ring from his suitcase and headed back to Jansen, who was now on her feet.

"Jansen, we're not over." He opened the ring box and held it out to her. "We do have a future."

She gasped at the beauty of the stone. "What is this?"

"The ring that should've been on your finger years ago."

"You've been holding on to this all these years?"

He nodded and took her hand in his and stroked her ring finger. "Jansen…"

"Bradley, we can't relive the past, no matter how good it feels. I know you think your apology changes things, but it doesn't. You broke my heart. You made me feel as if I had betrayed you because I wanted to go after my dreams."

"I know I was wrong, but don't you think we should make things right?"

She walked over to the door, grabbed her discarded dress and pulled it on. Bradley shook his head. "I'm not letting you walk away—again."

"I'm already gone," she said. "What's changed? What's different today from three years ago?"

"I'm different," he said.

"I don't believe you and I'm not taking that risk again." She stepped into her shoes and walked out the door.

Bradley grabbed his robe and started to chase after her, but then he sat on the edge of the bed. Had he really lost her again?

Chapter 8

Jansen stepped out onto the street and fought the urge to run. Though she felt horrible about leaving Shelby's brunch, she couldn't deal with the aftermath of what she and Bradley had done.

She also couldn't deny that she was still in love with that man and making love to him had confused her so much.

Closure. Yeah. Right. What if Bradley came out the door right now and saw the tumult of emotions flowing through her? She was wrong for having sex with him and walking away. How could she truly walk away when being in his arms brought back so many feelings and reminded her that she had never gotten over him?

Just keep in mind that your life is in New York now, she told herself as she headed down the street for the taxi stand. This was one time when she longed for a NYC Yellow cab. But the more she waited to see if

Bradley was going to show up, the more she simmered with anger and disappointment. "Typical," she muttered as she stood at the stand. "I don't even know why I'm upset. This is what Bradley does. It's his way or no way."

Folding her arms across her chest, she was almost ready to send Shelby a gift and go back to New York. Then she remembered Donovan's show, which was why she'd planned to leave Shelby's brunch early to begin with. Gritting her teeth, she prayed that she and Bradley could avoid each other now. The awkwardness should be gone now—or amplified tenfold.

How could she look at him now and pretend that they'd simply had a casual encounter and she was ready to go back to living as if they weren't tied together anymore?

She glanced over her shoulder again, hoping to see Bradley coming her way. When she didn't see him and heard an impatient driver yelling for her to get in the taxi or move, Jansen hopped into the cab and dropped her head, disappointed in her actions and Bradley's inaction.

Bradley made it to the taxi stand in time to see Jansen's cab pulling away. "Shit," he muttered.

"Monsieur?" the taxi-stand manager said.

"Nothing," Bradley replied. "Do you know where that lady is heading?"

The manager folded his arms across his chest. "Lady troubles? She left you?"

Bradley nodded. "I just need to return her diamond bracelet," he said. "She's friends with my sister, who's getting married in a few days."

The man eyed Bradley suspiciously. "Honest," Bradley replied. "My sister is going to kill me if she doesn't show up to the wedding with that bracelet."

He nodded in agreement with Bradley. "Women and weddings. They should focus on the marriage."

"Preaching to the choir. So, where's that taxi going?"

"Hotel Molitor."

Bradley reached into his pocket and handed the manager a wad of cash. "That's where I need to go."

The manager waved for the driver of the taxi that was next in line to take a group of passengers to the airport to drive Bradley where he needed to go first.

As he rode to the hotel, Bradley wondered if Jansen had meant what she said. Closure. Not on her life. That meant the end. Today was only the beginning.

"I'm not going to let her little tantrum stand," he muttered as the taxi pulled in front of the hotel. Though he knew tipping Paris taxi drivers wasn't a requirement like in the States, he handed the driver a couple of euros as he exited the car. When he walked into the lobby, he saw Jansen stepping into the elevator.

Sprinting toward her, he placed his foot in the door, preventing the elevator from closing. "Jansen," he said breathlessly. "I hope you didn't think we were done."

Shock clouded her face. "How did you…"

"Jansen, the last time you walked out on me I sat there. I knew you were coming back. You didn't. So, I would've been insane to let it happen again."

"Why don't we be honest with ourselves? We had a need and a desire, we satisfied it and it's over and done with."

He squeezed into the elevator and drew her into his arms. "That's a lie and you know it. Nothing is over between us."

"Let me go," she said, her voice a near moan. The last

thing she wanted was for him to let her go. She wanted to melt with him, to be his again. But her heart wasn't ready to take a chance on Bradley again. Not when she wasn't sure if what they shared in his hotel room meant as much to him as it did to her. She had made love to Bradley with her entire soul, and if he felt anything less than that, she wouldn't be able to handle the devastation.

He pulled her closer, brushed his lips across hers and stared into her eyes. "I feel your heart racing," he whispered. "It matches mine. We're not over."

"Bradley, let me—" He brought his mouth down on top of hers, kissing away any protest she'd been trying to mount. She lost herself in the kiss, wrapping her arms around his neck. Jansen moaned and wished they weren't in a camera-filled elevator.

"Still want me to let you go?" he whispered when they broke the kiss. "Still think we're done?"

"I—I…" The doors of the elevator opened and Jansen looked at the floor number. "This is my stop."

"All right, let's finish this in your room…"

"Jansen!" a young woman called out. "Where have you… Oh. Hello," she said when she looked at Bradley. "No wonder you forgot your fitting is in an hour."

"Shit," Jansen muttered. "I can't believe I booked the fitting at the same time I was supposed to be at Shelby's brunch."

"And," the woman continued with a smile, "Donovan's so excited about the wedding dress."

Bradley blanched. "Wedding dress?" he questioned. "I thought you said you weren't engaged?"

"We're going to have to talk about this later," she said. "I have to go. Dove, do you have the address?"

"Yes, and I called a car service for you. The driver should be waiting." She looked at Bradley, clearly still trying to figure out the weird energy between the two of them.

"Bradley, I'll stop by your hotel when I'm done."

"When you're done getting fitted for your wedding dress, you expect me to sit around and wait for you?"

Dove tapped her watch. "Jansen, we have to go." Jansen turned to Bradley.

"I'm sorry," she said, then she and Dove took off down the hall.

Bradley stood there simmering in anger. So, Jansen was that girl now? A lying cheater? Maybe she wasn't the same Jansen Douglas he'd fallen in love with in Atlanta.

His Jansen wouldn't have lied about a fiancé and made love to him while promised to another man. Then again, if she was able make love to him the way she did, pouring out every emotion into that bed, then she didn't love this man she was pretending to marry. "Why is she doing this?" he wondered aloud as he finally headed to the elevator.

Had she changed that much? Shaking his head, he wasn't ready to believe that. Heading back to his hotel, Bradley knew one thing for sure, he had to get to the bottom of Jansen's so-called relationship.

Chapter 9

"Who was the hottie in the hotel?" Dove asked for the third time as she and Jansen walked into the salon where Donovan had set up shop.

"What part of *I don't want to talk about it* don't you understand?" Jansen snarled.

Dove threw her hands up. "All right, but this is so not like you. He must be someone pretty important."

Jansen stopped in the middle of the doorway and glared at her assistant. "Since you want to get all up in my personal business, why don't you tell me about you and Donovan."

Dove's face turned a deep shade of red. "Um, I…"

"Glad you ladies could join me," Donovan said as he walked into the salon. Jansen didn't miss the wink between him and Dove, but she didn't want to say anything because that would open up a path to more questions about Bradley.

"Sorry I'm late," she said.

"No problem, it's Paris and a beautiful day. I was almost late myself," Donovan said, then ushered her over to the fitting area. "I had to finish this, though." He nodded toward the ivory gown hanging on a mannequin. Jansen's breath caught in her chest at the beauty of the lace-and-silk dress. Strapless with a heart-shaped neckline, crystals weaved into the bodice making the dress look as if it had been frozen. An ice princess bride. It was beyond a fairy-tale dress, it was fit for a queen and Jansen couldn't wait to put it on.

"You've truly outdone yourself," she said in admiration.

"I won't know that until you put it on. I made this with your measurements and figure in mind," he said as he cautiously removed the dress from the mannequin.

Jansen started to strip out of her dress, then she remembered she wasn't wearing underwear. Donovan pointed toward the dressing room. Jansen rushed in and stripped down so that she could put the dress on. She was careful not to cause any of the crystals to fall off. When she finally had the dress on, she spun around and felt like a princess.

"Come out, let's see it!" Dove called out.

Jansen pulled the curtain back and strutted out. "Woo," Dove exclaimed. "You and that dress are meant for each other. Somebody call a preacher."

"Come over here into the light," Donovan said, motioning toward the open space in front of the wide windows. "Yes." He held Jansen out an arm's length away. "Breathtaking. You're the showstopper."

She smiled broadly then turned toward the window and saw Shelby, Bradley and Jacques looking inside at them.

* * *

Bradley's jaw dropped as he drank in Jansen's image in that wedding dress.

"Oh my God," Shelby said. "Is that Jansen? Is this why she skipped my brunch? That dress is everything, though."

"I have to go," Bradley said as he took a fleeting look at his woman standing there in a wedding dress in the arms of another man.

"No," Shelby said, grabbing his arm. "You can't run…"

"I'm not running, but I'm not about to stand here and look at that."

"You know what, Bradley. Maybe you deserve this, deserve to see her happy because you let her walk out of your life and have done nothing to make up for it. Was she supposed to wait for you forever?"

"Did I say that?" Bradley snapped, feeling the punch of his sister's words. Maybe he'd expected Jansen to wait because he had. He knew he would never love another woman the way he loved her.

"Let's go, Jacques," Shelby said, linking arms with her fiancé. "And tell Jansen that I'm still salty about her absence at my brunch." Then she turned back and glanced at her brother. "Until she has a wedding ring on her finger, it's not too late to do something."

Bradley stood there and locked eyes with Jansen as she turned toward the window. Did she really lie to him about getting married? He damn sure was about to find out.

Jansen was transfixed by Bradley's stare from the other side of the window. What was he doing there? How had he found her? Was it fate?

"There he is again," Dove said. "What's the deal, Jansen?"

Just as she was about to open her mouth, the door opened and Bradley walked in. "I've never seen a more beautiful bride," he said. "Although, I'm a bit confused."

"How—what are you doing here?" Jansen asked.

Bradley smiled. "It just so happens that Shelby and her fiancé wanted to take me sightseeing and I saw you standing in this window. I guess the rumors are true," he said as he walked over to her. "And you lied to me. I can't believe you're that woman now."

"What?" Donovan said.

"Can we have a moment?" Jansen said, turning to Dove and Donovan. Her face burned with anger at Bradley's accusation.

"Sure, but can you take the dress off first?" Donovan said, throwing his hands up.

Jansen nodded and slipped into the dressing room. As she removed the dress, she heard Dove pressing Bradley for information.

"How do you and Jansen know each other?" her assistant asked.

"We go way back," he said.

"Are you stalking her?"

Jansen pulled on her dress and headed out into the salon. "Dove, it's all right. Bradley's Shelby's brother and he's not a stalker. He's safe." *Except where my heart is concerned.*

"I'm just looking out for you, boss lady. Donovan and I are going to go for croissants now. That place around the corner that we passed on the way in." She linked arms with the designer and they headed out the door, leaving Bradley with a confused look on his face.

"So, he's truly not your fiancé?" Bradley asked, feeling like the biggest fool in France.

Jansen speared him with an angry stare. "Do you really think I would've made love to you if I was getting married? Oh, but I'm that *woman* now. If that's what you really think about me, why are you here?"

"What was I supposed to think when I walk by and see—"

"I'm a model, I wear wedding dresses all the damn time. I work with a lot of designers who actually like—no, love—the way I look in their clothes. Some of them are men, and, yes, some of them will hug me."

"I'm sorry, Jansen," he said, drawing her into his arms. "But after all the press about you two and then seeing you in his arms…"

"Shut up! I can't believe you," Jansen said. "I'm not going to play this game with you. If you loved me, then you should've let me know a long time ago." Tearing away from him, Jansen turned her back to him and let her tears fall.

"Where do we go from here?" he asked.

"You think I'm a liar and the worst kind of woman. So, why the hell would you want a future with me?" she asked without turning around. She was afraid that if he looked into her eyes, he'd know she was lying. That she was simply allowing her pride to speak for her. "After Shelby's wedding, we can just go back to the way things were. You live your life and I live mine."

"That doesn't work for me."

"It's not always about what you want. Then again, that's why we're not together."

"I was wrong! I see that now and I can admit it. I'm sorry. But I'm not going to pretend that I don't love you and want you in my life again. You can lie to yourself,

Jansen, but don't lie to me. You still love me and there's no way that either of us can pretend that we don't deserve another chance to be happy—together."

"There you go calling me a liar again," she said. "I'm not going to change to fit into the mold that you have for your life partner. We're different people now. I'm about growth and teaching other women that they don't have to give their power away. I'm not about to go back to supporting your dreams while mine fall to the wayside."

"I'm not asking you to do that. And while I see that you have grown into a phenomenal woman, at the end of the day, we're still the same people who shared my mother's lasagna and fell in love."

She turned and faced him. "No, we're not, Bradley. My career, my future, it matters to me. Can you say the same? Do you still think that this was some act of frivolity I engaged in because I was bored at the family-life center?"

"No. Jansen, I know I was wrong and I want you to—"

"I can't do this. I can't pretend we have a future when you haven't given me a reason to believe you're different. My life's in New York and you're still living your life in Atlanta. We missed our chance and it's time to put the past behind us."

"We can put the past behind us. But I'm not writing off our future."

Jansen looked into his eyes and wanted nothing more than to fall into his arms and tell him how much she'd dreamed of a future with him. But she couldn't. And there was her business to think about.

"Come back to me, Jansen," Bradley whispered.

"Are you going to stand by me and support my dreams now?"

"Yes."

"For how long?"

"Why do you keep expecting the worst from me?" he asked.

"That's what you gave me and I'm not setting myself up for a repeat performance!" She pounded her fist against his chest, her tears free-falling.

Bradley grabbed her wrists and pulled her closer to him. He captured her mouth in a slow kiss; her sweetness mixed with salty tears nearly brought him to his knees. He didn't know he'd hurt her this much. Bradley didn't care if it took the rest of his life, he was going to make it up to her.

"Jansen," he moaned when they broke the kiss. "I'll never hurt you again."

"My life is in New York. I'm not…"

"I want to be wherever you are, New York, Atlanta, Paris, just say where."

She shook her head. "What about the center? And don't tell me you can give it up, because I know how hard you fought to keep it open."

"I never said I'd give it up. But who says I can't have both?"

She nodded. "I've always been proud of the work you do there. And—"

"I wanted you by my side. I just went about it the wrong way. But after the fight with Kenyon and Shelby, I needed someone on my side. I thought it was going to be you. In that moment when you were about to start your journey, I was lost. Jansen, I need you. I need you more than you will ever know."

She closed her eyes and sighed. "Why didn't you tell me that then?"

"Would you have stayed?"

She dropped her head, not knowing how to answer that question. If Bradley had asked her to stay in Atlanta that day, would she have been able to do it? Jansen raised her head and looked at him. "Maybe. If you needed me that much, maybe I would've stayed."

"And given up something that's obviously important to you? Look at what your career has led to. And you've given a voice to so many faceless victims of violence."

"You thought I was just going to get caught up in the glitz and glamour and forget about the victims we were charged with helping," she said, echoing part of what he'd said in their argument that day.

"I was wrong—about so many things. I get that now, and I know I can't make up for the past, but we can have a better future, Jansen."

She stroked her forehead. "Why did it take all of this, all of these years for you to say what I needed to hear then?"

"I know. We should be celebrating our anniversary instead of having this awkwardness between us."

She pushed out of his embrace. "It's been fun reminiscing with you, but I have to go." Dashing out of the salon, Jansen caught up with Donovan and Dove at a sidewalk café.

"Everything all right?" Dove asked when Jansen stopped in front of the table. Jansen shook her head and took an empty seat beside Dove.

"Donovan," she asked. "When's your fashion show?"

"It's been pushed back about a week. What's wrong, and don't say nothing, because you're frowning and models don't frown. Especially not you."

"I have to get away. I promised that I'd do the show, but I can't stay here."

Dove and Donovan exchanged glances. "Is this about Mr. Hottie, who's coming this way right now?" Dove asked as she looked over Jansen's shoulder.

"Damn it," Jansen muttered.

"It would be nice if you'd stop running," Bradley said, ignoring the people staring at them.

"I'm not running," she said, rising to her feet. Bradley looked at her with a raised eyebrow. Donovan shot Bradley a questioning look.

"Hey, brother, this is kind of weird because it looks to me like Jansen doesn't want to be bothered right now," Donovan said.

"It's all right," Jansen said, noticing the tightening of Bradley's jaw. "Bradley's going to leave."

"No, I'm not. We can finish this here in front of an audience or we can talk in private—either way, we're doing this."

She shook her head. "There's nothing left to do." Jansen grabbed her purse. "Tell Shelby I'm sorry, but I won't be at the wedding." She tore off running down the street. When Bradley started to follow her, Donovan hopped over the railing and grabbed his arm.

"Don't know what's going on, but give her some space. Let her calm down," he said.

"Get your hands off me." Bradley snatched away from him.

"Look, man, I'm guessing that you're not some stalker fan and you two have history, but let the lady breathe for a second."

Dove crossed over to the men as if she could sense the tension between them. "Guys," she said, "I know Jansen, and if she needs a moment, let her have it. I'm

going to call her and make sure everything is all right."
She turned to Bradley. "What did you do to her?"

"Let her walk out of my life, and I'm not going to
let it happen again."

Dove brought her hand to her mouth. He was the
one. "Wait—Bradley Stephens. Oh my... I should've
put it together."

He furrowed his brows and looked at her as if wings
had sprouted from her shoulders. "What do you mean?"

"I've heard some things about you, good and bad.
And for you two to reconnect in Paris. There's something old Hollywood about it," Dove said as she clasped
her hands. She turned to Donovan and smiled. "Maybe
we should see if we can help them. After all, we're in
the most romantic city in the world."

Donovan stroked her arm. "We should mind our
business."

Bradley grabbed a napkin from the table and wrote
his number down on it, then handed it to Dove. "I'm
going to catch up with my sister. If you hear from Jansen, tell her to call me."

Donovan took the napkin before Dove reached for it.
"Like I said. We're going to mind our business."

Bradley decided that it was best for him to leave
rather that do something he'd later regret. Heading up
the street, he was surprised to see Shelby and Jacques
standing outside another café. The look on his sister's
face told him that she wasn't happy. The last thing he
needed was Shelby's drama right now.

"You!" she snapped when she spotted her brother.
"What did you do to her?"

Jacques tapped his fiancée's shoulder. "Calm down,"
he whispered in French.

"Non!" Shelby pointed her manicured finger at him.

"Jansen said she's not coming to my wedding, and I know it has something to do with whatever you said to her in the salon back there."

"All I said to her was that I love her. Where did she go?"

"Wait. What? You told her that?" Shelby's scowl turned into a smile. "I'm glad you came to your senses."

"Where is she?"

"Probably at her hotel booking a flight out of here. She made me promise not to tell you, and you can't go after her now!"

"Maybe I can stop her from leaving. Jacques, give me your keys."

"What?" he asked, a befuddled look clouding his dark and handsome face.

"Nope," Shelby said as she snatched the keys from her fiancé. "I'm getting married in three days. This is not happening! Besides, Jansen needs a chance to get her head together."

"Did she tell you that?" Bradley asked, seconds from losing his patience and ripping the keys from his sister's hand.

"No, but don't you think this is a lot for her to take in? You breezing into her life telling her what she needed to hear years ago. I'd go to Jamaica, too. Oh, *merde*."

"Jamaica?" Bradley said, now wishing he'd taken Dove's number. He sprinted back down the street hoping to locate Jansen's assistant and find out where in the world Jansen took off to in Jamaica.

Jansen started to ignore the constant ringing of her cell phone as she hopped into a taxi to head to the airport. She had packed faster than a zebra running from a lion in the savanna. She wasn't running, she was just saving herself from another heartbreak. At least that's what she told herself. When she'd planned her new future, she hadn't expected that Bradley wanted a position in it. But could she trust that she wouldn't end up without him again?

After all, she thought he'd made this new life without her. *Why are you leaving?* her inner voice called out as she reached into her bag for her cell phone. When she saw that it was Dove, she hit the ignore button again.

She only needed a few days to think, and though the last-minute trip to her vacation home in Rio Nuevo was going to cost her a fortune, it was well worth it. As she reached the boarding gate, her phone rang again. Jansen knew she couldn't keep ignoring Dove.

"Yes, Dove?" she said, answering without looking at the caller identification.

"Sorry, it's Shelby," her friend said. "Jansen, I love you, girl."

"What did you do?"

"It was an accident, let me make that clear."

"Shell?"

"I accidentally told Bradley you were on your way to Jamaica."

"Damn it! If I wanted him to know, I would've invited him," Jansen growled.

The ticket agent gave her a confused look. Nodding at the woman as if to say everything was all right, she told Shelby she had to go.

"If you turn around and come to my wedding, you'll miss him."

"Goodbye, Shelby," she said as she handed the agent her boarding pass.

Chapter 10

Bradley stalked around his hotel room like a caged beast. Kenyon shook his head as he watched his brother. "You need to get your life together, brother," he said, then crossed over to the minibar and poured himself a drink. "She left, let it go. Sometimes everything isn't meant to be."

"Shut up."

Kenyon took a sip of his drink and shrugged. "She bolted on you. If that doesn't answer your questions, I don't know what will. So she's not engaged, but she isn't trying to start over with you, either."

"Shut up!" Bradley walked over to the minibar and poured himself a drink, as well. "What the hell am I supposed to do?"

"You have two choices."

Bradley raised his eyebrow at Kenyon as he spoke. "And they are...?" he asked.

"Go after her and maybe make a fool of yourself or

continue to be miserable and make the women of Atlanta miserable, then find yourself on an episode of *Snapped.*"

"You're annoying me. Where in Jamaica can she be?"

Kenyon took a seat on the sofa and shook his head. "How is it that I remember more about your woman than you do? Remember after the accident when we wanted to get away from the media and all the well-wishers?"

"Yeah, right before you sued me," Bradley said sarcastically.

"Are you ever going to let that go? How many times do I have to say I was wrong?"

"We went to…"

"Rio Nuevo," they said in concert. Bradley nodded.

"I bet that's where she's going. She loves that place," Bradley said.

"Before you go rushing off to Jamaica, don't you think you owe it to Shelby to stay here and walk her down the aisle, Mr. Family Values?"

"She called you already?"

He nodded and downed the remainder of his drink. "We came to Paris for our sister. After the wedding you can go after Jansen and try to have this idyllic life you think is still waiting for you."

Bradley knew he couldn't disappoint Shelby. After the wedding, he was going to get his woman back.

The next few days in Paris, Bradley felt as if he was in a daze. While his sister reveled in the festivities of the wedding—the parties, the dress fitting and more parties—he wondered if it would be like this for him and Jansen when they finally professed their love to the world.

By the time Shelby's wedding day rolled around, Bradley could only think of one thing as he walked his little sister down the aisle and into the arms of Jacques Luc, saying *I do* to Jansen.

All he had to do was convince her they belonged together.

Silence, except for the waves gently crashing against the shore, should've given Jansen peace. There were no cameras following her around Rio Nuevo, even though the tabloids had started telling the tale of Jansen's devastating breakup with Donovan and his relationship with her assistant. The fact that she and Donovan never had a relationship didn't get in the way of a good story. She'd counted her blessings for being able to avoid the paparazzi while in Paris. Lord knows she'd had a couple of public spats that would've filled the blogs and tabloids for days.

While Jansen was happy that Dove and Donovan had found each other, she wondered if it was true love or would Dove face a harsh heartbreak as she had with Bradley?

Was he for real now? Did he really love her and want a future together? Why hadn't she given him the chance that she knew he deserved? Fear.

"When did I become a coward?" she muttered as she shifted in the hammock. The wind blew over her and she sighed. There were only a few more days for her to wallow in her self-imposed paradise prison before she had to return to Paris for Donovan's show. Would Bradley still be there or had she run him off this time?

Rising from the hammock, she untied her sarong and walked toward the beach. A swim would clear her head, at least she hoped that it would. Diving into the clear blue water, she swam about a half a mile out from shore, then decided that she was a little too distracted for a long swim. She'd been thinking about Shelby's wedding and hoped that her friend would forgive her for not being there two days ago. There was no way she would've been able to watch Bradley in a tuxedo and not think of what could've been.

Stepping out of the water, she pushed her wet tresses off her forehead, and she must have been hallucinating because there was no way Bradley Stephens was standing on the steps of her cabana.

"Hello, Jansen," he said.

Now she was losing her mind, because the mirage was talking. Blinking, she realized that she wasn't seeing things. Bradley was here.

"How did you…"

"Jamaica. I remembered how much this place meant to you and how it helped us after Mom and Dad died. I meant what I said in Paris."

"You said a lot in Paris," she said with a smile. He stepped down and closed the space between them. She drank in his casual image, beige linen suit, brown leather sandals and Ray-Bans covering his eyes. Despite the shades, she felt his gaze roaming her wet body, clad in a red bikini.

"Red is your color," he said with an appreciative smile.

"Bradley, I'm sure you didn't fly all this way to tell me I look good in red." She stepped away from him and headed up the steps to retrieve a towel. He touched her elbow and stopped her in her tracks.

"When I walked Shelby down the aisle, I wondered what it would be like to be Jacques. Standing there waiting for the woman he loves to meet him at the altar and begin their life together. I was a little jealous."

"Why?"

"Because I'd run the woman I love away again. This

time, I knew I had to find you immediately," he said as he spun her around and held her against his chest. Her dampness seeped through his suit, but he didn't care. Just feeling her warmth against him caused his blood to heat. Bringing his lips against hers, he kissed her soft and deep. Jansen melted against his body, her loud doubts that brought her to Jamaica dulled to a quiet whisper as he nibbled her bottom lip.

Moaning, Jansen closed her eyes, almost feeling as if she was in the middle of one of her dreams. The moment she felt his hands stroking her back, she knew it wasn't a dream.

"Jansen," he moaned as he slipped his hands inside her bikini bottom. Cupping her behind, he brushed his lips across her neck. "I want our future."

"What?"

"Marry me." He kissed her neck and she shivered.

"I—I… What about the center? How are you going to run the center in Atlanta while I'm starting my business in New York?"

Bradley smiled. "That's the good thing about a family business—you have help. And if New York is where you need to be, then I'm going to be right next to you." He rubbed his hands up her sides.

She smiled, her eyes filling with tears. "Bradley," she whispered.

He took her face in his hands and kissed her again. "I have never loved anyone as much as I love you. Jansen, you stole my heart and never gave it back."

"Bradley, I've tried to get over you. I wanted to believe that you'd moved on and had this family in Atlanta. I turned down several modeling gigs there because I didn't want to run into your wife or see a little boy running around Peachtree Street with eyes like yours."

"You were in no danger of seeing that because if I couldn't have that life with you, I didn't want it."

"And you want it now?"

He nodded. "I want it right now."

"How can we just—"

"Do you love me?" The heat from his breath sent shivers down her spine.

"Yes."

"Then, here's what we're going to do," he said. "Donovan and Dove are here with that dress you tried on in Paris. Shelby and Jacques Luc are making me pay for their honeymoon here and Kenyon is looking for a pastor or justice of the peace."

She tilted her head and glanced at him. "What are you saying?"

"That you'll be my wife by sunset. Let's go inside."

Jansen, though she was a bit confused, followed Bradley inside the villa and gasped when she saw Donovan and Dove standing there with the dress.

"What in the..."

"Congratulations," Dove said with a huge smile on her face. "When Shelby told me the story about you two, I had to help."

"And," Donovan said, "I can't think of a better way to premiere my wedding dress collection than having the Face actually get married in the showstopper."

"But you have to get cleaned up first," Shelby said as she walked in the front door. "And even though you dipped out on my wedding, I'm going to make sure you and jerk face over here make it down the aisle because you two are wearing me out!"

"Shut up, Shell," Bradley said.

Jansen shook her head, overwhelmed at everything that was going on. "We're really doing this?"

"Yes. Unless you can think of a reason why we shouldn't."

She wrapped her arms around him and kissed him. "No. Only that we should've done this a long time ago."

Shelby and Dove linked arms with Jansen. "Come on, let's go." While the ladies headed upstairs, Bradley and Donovan stood in silence.

Finally, Bradley got tired of just watching the designer when he had questions about the true nature of his relationship with Jansen. Before he could get his question out, Donovan laughed. "I know what you're thinking, and no."

"You and Jansen…"

"Are just business partners. I have to say she did inspire my latest line, and were it not for her, Dove and I would've never met. Trust me, if there was something between Jansen and me, I wouldn't have given up so easily. Maybe now the tabloids will move on to something else."

"I'll drink to that," Bradley said as he headed over to the bar in the corner of the room and pulled out a bottle of rum.

"How did you know following her here wouldn't leave you with egg on your face?" Donovan asked when Bradley handed him a glass of rum and cola.

"I didn't. But when you really love someone, you just have to take that leap of faith." The men clinked glasses.

"You'd better go get ready," Donovan said as he glanced at his watch.

"Thanks for bringing the dress. When I saw her standing in that wedding gown in Paris, I knew it wasn't too late."

Donovan laughed. "And you thought she was getting ready to marry me. Rule number one in being with the Face—don't believe anything you read."

"True that!" Bradley said, then headed outside to his car. If Kenyon found a pastor or justice of the peace, he would have his wish and be making love to his wife by the time the sun set.

"Is this really happening?" Jansen asked her friends as she smoothed gloss across her lips.

"The better question is—is this *finally* happening?" Shelby quipped as she toyed with her friend's hair.

"All this time I thought you were just superpicky, but if I had that man waiting for me, I would've been the same way," Dove said. She held up her phone and snapped a picture of Jansen as she stood up and looked at her reflection in the mirror.

"I had no idea he was waiting for me," she said.

"That's because you wouldn't let me tell you," Shelby said, then picked up her cell phone to snap a picture of her future sister-in-law. "Both of you have been miserable all this time and too damn stubborn to admit that you still love each other."

"Point taken, Shelby."

She was about to snap another picture, when she received a text message. "Well, it's time to meet your destiny," Shelby exclaimed. "They're ready for us."

Jansen's knees shivered. She was actually getting married to Bradley Stephens. When she paused, Shelby shot her friend a questioning look. "You're not having cold feet are you?"

"No. Let's do this," she said, then linked arms with her girls and headed for the beach.

Bradley watched his future dressed in white silk and lace coming his way. Jansen was stunning as she walked into his arms on the shores of the beach. He didn't wait until they were pronounced husband and wife to kiss her.

"Too soon, bro, too soon," Kenyon whispered as he tugged at his brother's arm. Everyone laughed.

"I see that this needs to be a quick service," the pastor said.

"This has been a long time coming," Bradley said as he took Jansen's hands in his. They faced each other and the sun cast a halo around them.

"Yes, it has," she replied.

"Everything happens in God's time," the pastor said. "And what a day the Lord has made as two souls become one. Bradley Stephens, do you take Jansen Douglas to be your lawfully wedded wife?"

"I do," Bradley replied, then kissed her palm.

The pastor focused on Jansen. "Now, Jansen Douglas, do you take Bradley Stephens to be your lawfully wedded husband?"

She closed her eyes and a smile spread across her lips. "I do."

"Then, by the power vested in me, I *quickly* pronounce you husband and wife." Before the words *you may kiss the bride* escaped the pastor's lips, Bradley had his mouth on top of Jansen's, savoring the sweetness of her kiss and knowing that she would be his for the rest of their lives.

"I love you," he said. "Don't ever doubt that for a second."

"I never will again," she said.

Bradley scooped his wife into his arms and kissed her slow and deep. "Mrs. Stephens," he said when they broke the kiss, "are you ready to start our forever?"

"Mr. Stephens, I am so ready," Jansen said, stroking his smooth cheek.

* * * * *

For Tara Gavin—

I appreciate every moment of working with you.
Thanks for seeing my strength and potential when I couldn't. I
dedicate *Unraveled*'s quirky, beautiful, kick-ass heroine to you.

Dear Reader,

Don't do anything I wouldn't do. Have you ever said this to
someone? Do you really know what you would or wouldn't
do? I've said this quite often to friends when it comes to men,
but I never meant "Be cautious" or "Mind your morals."
Instead, I meant "Be brave. Be sweet. Be naughty. Because
that's what I would do." At least, that's what I thought before
I wrote *Unraveled*.

When I crafted Ona Tracy, I stranded her on an erotic-themed
cruise ship. I put myself in her stilettos, listed the things
I'd never do—and let Ona do those things. As this volatile
character took shape, I realized that I'm not as brave, sweet
or naughty as I thought. So when Ona experienced a carnal
awakening at the hands of rough-hewn ex-marine Riker Ewan,
I experienced an awakening of my own.

And I figured I'm overdue for a cruise…

XOXO

Lisa Marie Perry

UNRAVELED

Lisa Marie Perry

Chapter 1

She needed a drink. She needed it tall, she needed it straight and she needed it to go down hard and wear off slowly.

It was the only proper way to give her career a send-off. Ona Tracy knew that her shiny new gig as an event planner had already departed on its maiden voyage to hell. And it wouldn't be coming back.

To think she'd maxed out her platinum American Express card, straightened her hair to perfection and redeemed all of her airfare rewards points for a flight from New York to Miami for this. In Cartier Paris sunglasses, a gold-belted dark blue pinhole button-down dress and scarlet snakeskin pumps, clutching designer luggage from a Saks Fifth Avenue and Neiman Marcus binge she would be regretting had she not been backstabbed out of a cushiony advertising firm, she would at least look good when they crucified her.

The extravagant ship before her wasn't the cruise liner she'd booked for her high school glee club's ten-year reunion. And any moment now, the sixteen wealthy and entitled former Philadelphia Academy of Arts and Culture students and eight plus-ones due to arrive on the pier would know it.

Most likely to succeed, my ass. Ten years ago she'd taken pride in the yearbook superlative, had even been shallowly touched that the majority of over a hundred students had agreed that if anyone in their graduating class had a shot at taking what they wanted out of life, it was Ona.

Why not, anyway? The Tracys had a strange way of conquering the odds. In one spectacular year she'd gone from being a Fishtown working-class kid living on a predominately black street in Philly to being the only Fishtown working-class kid—and the only black girl—enrolled at PAAC, one of the most elite private high schools in the East. Vocals that might make angels ugly-cry and a dare to jump into a park fountain and belt out a show tune had led to the scholarship that had opened the golden doors of her education.

But she'd locked herself out the back exit by dropping out of Juilliard, declining the chance to understudy in a West End production and passing up a touring cast role in one of Broadway's longest-running shows. No one had told her to trade all her dreams for a man. No one had told her to believe in love.

No one had told her to repeat her mistakes over and over until she'd come to the point of falling from grace, dusting off her ass and persuading her alma mater to hire her to coordinate PAAC's glee club reunion.

Okay…she wasn't exactly the übersuccessful answer-to-your-prayers event planner she'd sold to school administrators. Technically she had zero professional experience. There was the dinner party she'd helped her ex-boyfriend host at his Park Avenue penthouse, but she hadn't gotten compensated—unless you counted thank-you sex so boring that she'd faked moans to hide yawns and had been relieved to be interrupted by his ringing business cell, which he'd had the audacity to answer before pulling out. Prior to that she'd arranged a Hamptons weekend baby shower for a Mommyzilla friend who'd dismissed her from the festivities after discovering the silk Ona had used to decorate the seven-tier diaper cake was Oxford blue, not periwinkle.

To say she had any genuine, concrete event planning experience, she had to go back—way back—to her days at PAAC. A moth among butterflies, she'd joined every committee she could in efforts to impress college admission committees while blending in with the Joneses. She'd made herself indispensable, a go-to person who tap-danced across the fine line between satisfying PAAC's precise expectations and secretly giving the students what they wanted. Unlike the rest of her high school colleagues, she hadn't been sheltered. She'd become the *after*-party girl—the one with the Philly connections and street smarts to shepherd her classmates to nightly off-campus freedom they wouldn't get under the control of a tyrannical headmaster and a council of wannabe puritans.

In a stroke of kooky Tracy luck, the powers-that-be had remembered her as a shining gold star student, but hadn't been brought up to speed on her musical theater crash and burn, nor her disastrous misadventures in cobbling together a career in advertising.

Not knowing that Ona Tracy had almost been a Broadway sweetheart, had almost ended up an advertising somebody, had almost been engaged and was an event planning virgin, PAAC had become her first real client.

And somehow, despite dressing the part and acting the part, she'd botched this, too. Making the most of the school's budget and sky-high expectations, she had cherry-picked *The Lore*, one of the Stewart-Russ Cruise Line's family-friendly vessels, for a weeklong trip to the Bahamas.

"*The Lore*, this ain't," she whispered to her designer suitcases full of secrets. What good would sexy lingerie and an economy-size bottle of lube be now when this trip and what she'd quietly hoped to reap from it were all but dead in the glistening green-brushed blue water?

The Lore, a classy and elegant ship she'd virtually toured on her do-it-all smartphone, was the smallest of the company's other general crafts. There was *The Legend* and *The Myth* and others she couldn't remember now as her heart palpitated, but she certainly hadn't reserved a specialty ship that boasted the image of a mystical tit-baring sea seductress.

Carved into the side of the gleaming gold-trimmed eggshell-white vessel were the words *The Lure*, followed by *Omnia Vincit Amor*.

No, no, no. A vowel mix-up couldn't possibly be the difference between a successful new career and yet another flop.

"Omnia Vincit Amor."

Arousal strapped itself to Ona. Nick. Nicholas Callaghan. Dark-haired, green-eyed perfection.

"'Love conquers all,'" she translated with a huskiness that wasn't so much sexy as it was raw.

"You know Latin, Ona?" Nick asked.

"I read *The Canterbury Tales*, same as you." Chaucer

was an institution at PAAC. She'd spent more energy daydreaming about Nicholas during AP English than translating text, but this, like her Christmas through New Year's weight gain, a girl kept on the hush-hush.

"Right." When his hand settled on her hip with a familiarity and gentle possessiveness that gave Ona naughty chills through her extremities, she pretended to concentrate on jostling her carry-on luggage in her arms to brace herself for the one-on-one reunion she'd been fantasizing about since finding his name on PAAC's glee club call list.

Beyond sharing an English class and the club, and exchanging perhaps a few sentences of small talk in all their time in high school, Ona and Nick had been strangers. In spite of her giving the ol' college try to fitting in, they'd existed on different planes. He was the descendant of a wealthy Irish family that owned the brewery that cranked out Ona's favorite beer. Ona's father drove delivery trucks and her mother taught piano. Had it not been for the gas-station everything-on-it hot dog and lucky lottery ticket Pa had bought while waiting for his rig's tank to fill one afternoon, the Tracys might still be rooted in Fishtown. Nick dated blondes and redheads. An African-American, Ona was as brunette as they came.

But she'd wanted him anyway—in unreachable, limitless ways she hadn't quite understood until she'd discovered the yummy "depravity" of unscrambled adult TV programming. Every sex act she'd viewed, every shock and thrill that did funny things to her adrenaline, she wanted to mimic with Nicholas. Not that she'd ever, ever let him know what was up. It was a risk she had never let herself attempt, and it had felt safe. After graduation she'd pushed the teenage crush way down

deep, had continued to walk on the safe side of life by
stepping out of the spotlight of unpredictable showbiz
and stepping into the shadows of relationships with men
who claimed to love her but were in actuality threatened by her potential for success.

Now Nick was twenty-eight and single, and so was
she, and the want was stirring awake after a ten-year
slumber.

Seducing Nick was supposed to be Ona's biggest
risk—her wildest dare since launching herself into a
Philadelphia park fountain and tearing into "And I Am
Telling You I'm Not Going."

If the tricks in her suitcases—lingerie and bikinis
that looked like lingerie—failed to stoke his interest,
she was prepared to trigger his jealousy by allowing
Matthew "Matty" Grillo, her best friend in high school
and the only soul who'd known of her nasty schoolgirl
crush, to pretend to be her man. It'd been Matty's sug-
gestion when she'd reached his name on the glee club
call list and, after years of no contact, they'd talked as
though they hadn't skipped a beat since getting wild
in the school auditorium and getting hot in the cos-
tume closet.

*I think you should go for it. Take a chance on him.
Hold nothing back. If Nick's crazy enough to not take
the ticket you're selling, and it means that much to you,
I'll screw you. That's a promise,* Matty had said in that
casual, sardonic way she'd come to miss over the past
decade.

You don't make promises, she'd pointed out, smiling
because even from Alaska where he'd given up singing for bush flying, Matty Grillo could make her smile.

Not the ones I don't plan to keep.

Silly thing was, it wouldn't happen. Sex wasn't an aspect of their friendship they couldn't pick up as though rediscovering a once-cherished toy in the attic. It wasn't something they could resume without skipping a beat.

Even though Ona had lost various virginities to Matty throughout high school, and sex had been a great perk to their friendship, clearly they were meant to be no more than friends. But she loved Matty, and she needed a reunion with him as much as she needed one with Nicholas.

"Ona," Nicholas said, drawing out the second syllable as his hand went lax on her hip, "this isn't the ship on the reservations."

"What gave it away? The *o* and *u* thing?"

"No, the naked mermaid. Are we at the right pier?"

"Yes—"

"Then the wrong ship is in front of us!" interrupted Regan Waltz, prying them apart with her bold summery perfume and the crack of her skinny high heels on the pier. Brandishing her phone, she continued, "I just did some fast research, and guess what? *The Lure* is a luxury ship. A special type of luxury ship."

By now others had flocked to the pier, following Regan as many had in high school. Like Nicholas's good-boy attractiveness and Matty's ability to put Ona at ease, some things hadn't changed.

"I realize that," Ona said calmly to Regan.

"Tell everyone exactly what it is, then."

Oh, hell naw. Ona had dealt with enough divas in musical theater to not buckle under one of Regan's tantrums. Addressing the gathering, she said, "Most of the Stewart-Russ Cruise Line's crafts serve a standard purpose…but this one is, um, it's a bit unique. It's called a specialty ship. It's…well, it's an erotic-themed ship, in case any of you couldn't figure that out by the sexed-up bare-breasted mermaid painted on the side."

"PAAC's not going to stand for this." Regan scowled at Ona. "I took vacation time for this event and it's ruined. We voted you Most Likely to Succeed. Should've been Most Likely to Screw Up Reunion. Figures, the nouveau riche are typically victims of mediocrity. You can take the girl out of Fishtown…"

"I thought you should've been voted Most Likely to Screw Her Way to the Top, but life's unfair like that," Ona snapped. As the apples of Regan's pale cheeks blossomed pink and she snapped glares at the chuckling crowd, Ona began to muscle her luggage toward *The Lure*. "Everyone hasn't arrived yet. If you'll all just wait here, I'll try my damnedest to correct this. I'm sure the ship's concierge staff can help us find a solution."

Such confidence, but inside Ona was miserable. Putting Regan Waltz in check had been a necessary move, but with the woman gunning for her, she had no chance of getting out of this unscathed. In high school, Regan had been half of every power couple, had unofficially reigned over their class. She had a take-charge presence that Ona had envied but accepted, just as she'd accepted that the others could see only what they wanted from Ona without actually seeing her.

She'd been Miss At-Your-Beck-and-Call, and as she hurried to the ship before the group could get on a conference call with PAAC, it dawned that she remained at their beck and call. Ten years hadn't changed the dynamics. They were still successful and entitled. In clothes she couldn't afford and no career to return to in New York, she was still a pretender.

Catching wind of the complaints swirling in the sultry April air, a pier staff member escorted Ona aboard the ship. Reservations and ID examined, luggage scrutinized, she was rushed to Guest Services. On the way, she fell momentarily speechless. Exotic extravagance swallowed her. Polished marble, touches of gold and platinum blended into the architecture and decor, spiral staircases embellished with crystal, intoxicatingly fragrant flowers—it all carried her into a reality that was almost magical compared to the crowded pier full of travel-weary and pissed off former private school classmates awaiting her.

"Welcome aboard *The Lure*," the man said belatedly. "I'm certain Guest Services will resolve your complaint, but I should tell you that the shipboard staff and the pier staff have communicated extensively and reviewed every accommodation in anticipation of your party."

"But this isn't the ship I reserved," she said through tightly locked teeth. "There's no logical way that my budget paid for all this. I browsed this ship online. It's quintessential luxury. And it's an erotic ship. Why would a private school okay an erotic reunion cruise for its glee club?"

"If you'd like," he said patiently, "I can request complimentary refreshments for your guests while we wait for a boarding decision."

"By 'refreshments,' do you mean liquor?"

"Our finest."

"Excellent. Do that." It wouldn't completely remedy the situation, but in her experience, if anything could pacify the wealthy and influential it was being reminded that they were wealthy and influential.

Inside the guest services manager's office suite, Ona was offered her own fine refreshment in a champagne flute and invited to relax on a sensual red tufted chaise and explain her dilemma.

It was supposed to be the Stewart-Russ Cruise Line's dilemma, but the shipboard staff weren't quite registering this.

"We require forty-eight hours' notice for group cancellations," the guest services manager, Quinn, said once Ona took a tentative sip of the champagne. Not that she didn't still need a drink—she so did—champagne just wasn't what she had in mind. "You reserved seventeen cabins, ma'am. Eight spa suites and nine of our most ideal staterooms. As much as our cruise line would like to issue a refund, it's simply against our policies."

"This isn't a cut-and-dry cancellation request," Ona clarified.

"Are you no longer interested in traveling to the Bahamas?"

"Yes, of course we are."

"Then, please understand I'm having trouble understanding the nature of your complaint."

"The nature of the complaint is I didn't reserve seventeen cabins on *The Lure*. I reserved *The Lore*, one of your standard ships. I'm traveling with sixteen of my high school classmates. About half of them come with significant others."

"This ship is known to be instrumental in helping singles explore their sexuality and for rejuvenating couples' relationships."

"Wh-what? No, we were in glee club together. We sing and dance. I mean, we used to, in high school. The point is we're not interested in exploring sexuality or rejuvenating anything." Ona stalled, tasting the lie flavoring her protests. She was interested in exploring her sexuality—particularly Nicholas Callaghan's role in it. "This isn't the ship I reserved. In fact, some of the guests in my party find the idea of this ship to be off-putting."

"Miss Tracy, our records indicate that you electronically signed a confirmation document that names *The Lure* as your cruise liner of choice. I'll print you a copy."

Oh, damn it, it was her fault. With two strikingly different ships bearing similar names, she reasoned it was an honest and understandable mistake. Yet— "I can't believe that the costs of a weeklong Bahamas cruise on *The Lore* are the same as they'd be on this ship."

Quinn presented the confirmation form, adding, "I'll take that to mean the discounted group rate was generously affordable at the time that you booked the reservations. As this isn't a Stewart-Russ error and policies prohibit us from refunding canceled reservations on such short notice, would you and your guests reconsider joining us? Boarding is open, but won't remain open for much longer."

"Wait—could we be switched to a different ship?"

"I'm afraid that's not possible. The itineraries are already in place."

"What about my itineraries?"

"Assuming you mean Nassau shore excursions and a ballroom reservation for Friday night? It's all here. I expect you'll immensely enjoy our shipboard pianist and four-piece orchestra." She began typing on her keyboard, then swept up a tablet. "In light of the confusion, our company has prepared a disclosure agreement that we'd like each member of your party to sign, should you decide to board. This is an adults-only ship and it's important that everyone understand some of the, er, special features."

"Such as?"

"The main deck is clothing optional. *The Lure* offers

sexually oriented workshops and events. There's a boudoir photographer. Features along those lines." She hastened to add, "We ensure our guests safety. Recording devices are prohibited in the workshops and electronic devices discouraged on the clothing-optional deck. The ship is secured with discreet specialists. And also along the lines of safety, we value our guests' health and employ board-certified physicians and a pharmacy."

"What don't you offer?"

"Pet care. No animals allowed."

Ona nearly confessed she wasn't offended by the restriction, since she was sadly allergic to anything with fur. But she wouldn't let *The Lure*'s glamor nor allergy-sufferer-friendly environment seduce her.

"My colleagues will be happy to assist in the check-in process, but the disclosures must be signed prior to boarding."

"One of our tenors became a corporate attorney." Ona threw it out there, thinking of wheelchair-bound Rajon Sneed, one of two black guys in glee club and one of five black guys in their class. Technically he was a disability rights advocate, but he swam in the right ponds and she wanted to know how this unflappable manager would respond to the soft threat.

"Please, encourage your attorney to review the document carefully. Our attorney is easily accessible. Perhaps they'd like to compare notes."

"Ha." Damn it again. It didn't seem conceivable that she'd made this blunder, but all the facts indicated the blame rested on her own ineptness and negligence.

"So either we board this ship or cancel our trip to the Bahamas and lose the money that the Philadelphia Academy of Arts and Culture invested?"

"Stewart-Russ supports you in whichever option you choose."

Obviously. Stewart-Russ wouldn't lose any funds in the transaction and wouldn't be held responsible for the scandal of a prestigious private school's glee club being reunited on a sex-themed cruise ship.

Ona returned to the pier and called on her dusty acting techniques to optimistically persuade her classmates to consider herding onto the ship. "None of us live in Florida," she reasoned. "We all traveled this far to go to the Bahamas together. I accept full responsibility, and I'm sorry, but this is our ship. It's a spectacular craft and this trip is going to be whatever we make of it."

Regan Waltz huffed and murmured something to those in her vicinity. "PAAC won't be pleased about this. Imagine what people will say."

"Let PAAC be displeased after the trip. If this is a reunion, then let it be a legitimate remember-when, just-like-old-times event, all right?" Ona's gaze touched the faces she remembered from her adolescence. "Remember all those nights I led you around Philly? You trusted me to show you something different—some adventure. Trust me this time."

Collectively, they hesitated.

"I've never seen a ship decorated with platinum before I walked aboard *The Lure*. I wouldn't want to travel to the Bahamas in anything but the best."

Regan's head cocked to the side, for a moment resembling a curious dog. "Platinum?"

"Crystal staircases. Champagne readily available. Things to never let you forget for a second that this is a vacation. I came to Miami for a vacation and to reconnect with the club. If we can all agree on that, I say we board before the ship departs without us."

"I can do that," Nicholas said, and Ona was proud of herself for refraining from melting on the pier or blurting how much she'd like him to pry open her pin-hole dress.

The others began trickling toward the ship and Ona hung back, apologizing profusely and bargaining with a higher power that she'd be forever grateful if she never had to grovel to these people again. They were her peers, but carried arrogance and superiority. They brushed past her as though traveling by luxury ship was a favor to her. She could respect that some weren't comfortable with the prospects of erotic workshops and seeing nudity on deck or in a sauna, but participation wasn't mandatory and there was Nassau and its trea-sures to look forward to.

As the last few of her former classmates strode past, she said, "Can we get a head count? We're not all here. Where's Matthew Grillo?"

Regan glanced at Ona, her expression hollow, but she didn't stop walking. "Matty Grillo's dead."

Chapter 2

Her friend—her best friend from high school—was dead?

Ona grabbed a handful of Regan's fluttery Prada sleeve. "Are you messing with me?"

"No, Ona. Get out your phone and fact-check. Matty died about ten days ago."

"You and I spoke last Monday. Why didn't you tell me about him then? He was my best friend from those days."

"The subject didn't come up in conversation. Everyone else knew. Guess you just weren't part of the loop—sorry. Besides, I didn't know you and Matty were like that. There was gossip about the two of you in high school, but what did I care if he was boffing a Fishtown girl?" Regan jiggled her arm free, tossed a look to the man behind her. "Cole, tell her the depressing details. I want to see what an erotic-themed ship's definition of a *stateroom* is."

Cole Stanwyck, who'd been the class ass with a bad case of grabby hands, removed his sunglasses but didn't dare prop them on his head and ruin his gel-spiked hair. "Stilts Tracy. Long time."

Not long enough… "Long time since anyone called me Stilts."

"I can fix that for you."

"I didn't say I missed the nickname. Just making the observation that lately I've been around people who don't feel the need to incessantly make me feel ashamed of my height. What do you know about Matty?"

"He crashed his bush plane in Alaska. It was quick. He didn't suffer."

"You're lying, Cole." Ona had stopped moving, but when he reached out to urge her along, she jerked. She hadn't wanted his hands on her in high school, and she didn't want them on her now. "If you'd kept your sunglasses on, I wouldn't see the lie in your baby blues."

"All right, then. The details I heard are this. Matty's plane was in pieces and so was he. It was up in flames before it blew, so he suffered like a son of a bitch."

"Oh, God. Matty…"

"I'm sorry he went out that way. But I didn't like Matty," Cole said darkly.

Who didn't like Matty Grillo? He was luminous, considerate, a straight-up smart-ass and one hell of a man.

Cole fell into queue behind her, and his breath on her ear had her body tensing violently—as it had when she was twelve and a Kensington crackhead had mugged her at gunpoint in broad daylight, and when she'd ended up alone with Cole in a music practice room at PAAC senior year. He couldn't see past the silver spoon up his butt, couldn't comprehend that white or black, rich or poor, no meant no. A violin upside his head had changed his attitude quick, and they hadn't seen each other in a decade, but his presence made her feel leerier than she'd suspected it would.

"Why didn't you like him?" Ona asked, shadowing the person in front of her just to dodge Cole's closeness.

"Because of you. What you had going on with him. You were wasting your time with him in high school, letting him pop you sophomore year and doing him when you could've been with me. He thought he could fly planes and wound up sprinkled across some Alaskan village. I've created three megasuccessful apps, own several million-dollar sports cars, and a private jet brought me to Miami. I'm at the top of my game. Think about joining me at the top."

Ona didn't want to be at the top of anything with Cole. The realization that he hadn't matured or grown out of his sleazy, self-important ways, and that she would be facing seven days at sea with him was depressing. Matty wouldn't be here to make Nicholas jealous or shield her from Cole. "No, thanks."

"Join me for a drink, then. What cabin are you in? I'll bring you what you like." When she shuddered, he asked, "What was that?"

I dry-heaved. It's a reflex—happens when smarmy men repulse me.

"Good for you that you've been living well, Cole, but I wasn't interested in high school and I'm not interested now. I hope you can respect that. Another thing—I loved Matty and I'm hurt that he's gone, so if you could also respect his memory, I'm sure a lot of us would appreciate that."

Cole put on his sunglasses. "You don't have to spend reunion crying over him when I'm here to make it bet-

ter. Or were you and Matty planning on having a reunion of your own?"

"It's not your right to know—" Ona scrambled to
think quickly as the person in front of her finished
checking in. Knowing that Ona was depending on
Matty, Cole would circle her relentlessly. He'd make
it a game—a hunt. "But I'll tell you anyway. I'm here
with someone. Matty was a friend and I'll miss him,
but I already have a man who'll help me deal with it."

The words were as genuine as a Manhattan street
vendor's twenty-dollar Gucci handbags, but she'd been
lying from the moment she presented herself as a ca-
pable professional event planner. It was harsh enough
that she'd spend reunion devastated by her friend's death
and that it'd occurred to none of her other classmates
or PAAC to notify her.

Hadn't everyone known that she couldn't have been
Most Likely to Succeed without Matty Grillo giving
her the friendship she'd needed to endure years in an
academy full of cutthroat schemers and old-money rich
kids whom she'd tried tirelessly to copycat? Even as she
respected them, she despised them. And even as she
despised them, she wanted to be one of them. Because
she hated being the unique one, the something new that
PAAC paraded about as though she were some diver-
sity ticket. Unlike the black males at PAAC, she wasn't
from money and was socially classified as at-risk. At
risk for teen pregnancy and drug use and poor academic
achievement and petty crimes—the same vexations several of her PAAC peers had met.

But "at-risk" Ona hadn't been one of them. She'd
been obsessively careful about sex, had never used
drugs, had kept up her grades and lived within the
boundaries of the law. She'd been good, safe, and was

now blindsided that being good and safe landed her here, facing a weeklong Bahamas cruise on an erotic ship with a group of people who didn't care about her enough to tell her that her friend's plane had crashed.

As Matty's best friend, she should've known about his tragedy. But…as his best friend, she should've been in his life during the ten years between graduation and a glee club call list phone conversation. They'd laughed, made stupid plans, and she'd thought they had picked up where they'd left off as if a decade had been no more than a blink. But the truth was they'd dropped the ball on their friendship, and she was left behind to mourn that, as well.

On board, Ona lost Cole as she put her sunglasses in her cross-body handbag and tipped a shipboard valet to take her luggage to her stateroom while she toured *The Lure*. Assuming most of her party would be eager to scope out their quarters—spa suites for the couples and staterooms for the singles—she figured she had a swell chance of reprieve from them and their complaints if she veered off elsewhere.

The place was more fascinating than a museum, more alluring than satisfaction. The staff wore silk and the air smelled like temptation.

Taking the first staircase, she ascended leisurely and allowed others to pass her because time no longer seemed to matter. Her feet were used to touching crumbling sidewalks, not steps made of crushed crystal. What wasn't dipped in gold was brushed with diamonds. With its black velvet ropes, erotic art, lustrous floors and blindingly magnificent chandeliers, and featuring entire rooms dedicated to everything from dancing to cigars to mediation to gambling, this ship was far more opulent than Stewart-Russ's standard cruise liners.

It was heaven for sinners, and not something the Philadelphia Academy of Arts and Culture would have approved of for its final cohort of glee club members. Ona and her classmates had sung with symphony accompaniment and at church charity functions, performed with celebrities and at Carnegie Hall, yet the club had been cut the summer after their graduation as investors shifted their interests to the school's athletics department. Glee club reunions weren't tradition at PAAC, but for sentimental reasons the school had created a treasury fund for the onetime event. A onetime event that Ona had turned into a mistake.

The most splendid mistake she'd ever make.

For seven days she wouldn't have to face PAAC. For seven days she wouldn't have to house-sit for her parents, who now filled their time experiencing great American wonders such as the Grand Canyon and Mount Rushmore. Seven days for seven capital sins, and *The Lure* promised to offer them all. For seven wicked, hedonistic days, she could be a successful, dare-thirsty, risk-hungry version of Ona Tracy.

At the top of the stairs, Ona ventured toward the gold-plated sign that indicated the upper deck. She could relax and watch the water for a while or sit someplace and check her email.

A doorman pushed open the door for her.

Nudity. In the pool, occupying almost every chaise longue, lining the safety walls, were naked men and women of various ages, ethnicities, heights and body types.

"Can I assist you?" the doorman asked, when she'd stood frozen in the entryway a moment too long. "Are you looking for a dressing room?"

"An *un*dressing room, you mean?" she muttered.

"Uh, no, thank you. I thought *clothing optional* suggested that some people might choose the clothing option."

"The lower deck best suits guests who want to keep their secrets to themselves," he said, but the slip of his gaze down her body revealed his regret that she was the lower deck type.

"I'll keep that in mind," she said, lurching back. "Sorry—really. It's just that nudity's new for me. Strangers' nudity. Publicly, out in the open. And as exhausting as this day has been for me, it's still too early in the afternoon for so much penis and vajayjay." Ona's sigh rode out on a frustrated growl. "I don't say *vajayjay.*"

"You just did. Twice."

Please, don't exert yourself being so helpful. "Are there any other naked watering holes on this ship? I'm here on a private school reunion and I'd like to lessen the impact of culture shock on the others if at all possible, you get me?"

Chuckling, he said, "The staff has been informed about your group. Use your discretion when visiting this deck and any closed doors marked VIP. Everything else should be tame."

"*Tame* tame or erotic-cruise tame?"

"The latter."

Ona's shoulders dropped. "Oh, hell."

"Ma'am? It's not my place, but this is your trip as much as it is theirs. *The Lure* encourages guests to have a personal experience. Now that you're on board, what would you like?"

The same thing she'd craved when she saw the ship and recognized her event planning career had capsized. "A drink. It's not too early for a rough drink."

"There's a bar near the lower deck. Take a moment to look at the virtual tour screens. There are several posted throughout the ship, and they're touch screen."

"No paper brochures?"

"Paper brochures are available, but I'm obligated to mention the new digital-age-friendly features. Take a chance on them."

"Take a chance?" Her mouth flattened and gravity and sorrow tugged the corners downward. "A friend of mine said something similar."

"Smart friend."

He should've been a smarter pilot, a safer man... He should be here to see a deck full of naked strangers and say something wry for her ears only, because they were once tight like that. He should be here to remind her that she'd survived PAAC and could survive this, too. He should just be, damn it.

Ona turned on her red snakeskin heel, edged aside as a couple she recognized from the staircase approached to access the clothing-unlikely deck. She tried to picture herself with the gall to strip and strut around where strangers could stare their fill, but all she got was empty space.

She'd had men before, and if she put her mind to it she could probably achieve most of the positions in the *Kama Sutra*, but she handled her body with care. For her, safe sex was about more than condoms—it was about sharing it with safe men.

The "safe" men she'd had serious relationships with in the past had fooled her. One had convinced her to drop out of Broadway because he predicted she'd cheat on him while on tour. The next had talked a big talk about marrying her, but his only true motive had been to wreck her career.

Nicholas Callaghan, a Rhodes scholar and a *Forbes*-featured millionaire, had all the right moves. He volunteered at a children's hospital and published a cookbook for diabetics. That degree of solidness, the transparency of his strong character, made him more appealing than any of the men in Ona's past. He wouldn't ask her to give up Broadway just because fame threatened his pride. He wouldn't tease her with engagement talk while he plotted to double-cross her out of one of Manhattan's top advertising firms. And he wouldn't move to Alaska and let ten years pass without hearing her voice. That was how safe Nicholas was, and Ona's determination to have him a little closer was as unyielding as cement.

A knight in spotless Armani. She'd take it. Because if she and Nicholas hooked up, then Cole Stanwyck would be an afterthought, not some uncontained threat short-circuiting her comfort.

Only, she hadn't expected interference in the form of a shipload of sexually jump-started guests. The chances of another woman capturing Nicholas's attention had grown exponentially. Her seduction plans had unraveled to nothing but a scatter of loose threads, and damn if she didn't deserve that drink.

Taking the same staircase down two flights, she roamed through rooms that looked like art galleries, pausing at a door ominously roped off with a pedestal before it that displayed in crisp, golden print *VIP*. Shaking off the impulse to court trouble, she located a tour guide screen mounted in a thick glass tower and sidled up to it with the intent of setting her course for the nearest bar.

Figuring this could take a minute, she stepped out of one high heel, then the other, and wiggled her toes before she fell into a slow, light dance of balancing her weight from foot to foot. Vaguely she was aware of a pair of denim-clad male legs on the opposite side of the tower, but she was so single-minded in her search that she didn't absorb the man's presence until she noticed that he was standing stock-still.

On instinct, she snapped her eyes straight ahead but found an interactive map on the LED screen. She glanced down again. His silver-buckled black belt down to his shoes, and heaven-sent denim in between, was all Ona could see. His feet were planted apart, his muscle-wrapped thighs encased in denim that was just snug enough to showcase a very male crotch.

That she couldn't take him in all at once intrigued her. She appreciated these drawn-out moments to consider the impression of the rod resting along his right thigh.

"Why did you stop moving?"

The question startled her, his voice so gruffly inviting that Ona tasted his words before she heard them. "Why are you standing there to begin with?" she asked, not breaking their pseudo-anonymity.

"There's a screen on this side of the tower, too."

"Why haven't you moved since you walked up to this tower?"

"You're hopping around in the middle of a hall…"

"And? There's an *and* floating here between us. A glass tower and an *and*."

"And your feet are the sexiest things I've seen on this ship."

Arousal rang through her—little bitty bells of horniness jingling throughout her body. She could get addicted to that voice. The dropped *r*, the touch of swagger in each syllable, gave him up as a Boston product, but his accent seemed residual, as though time away from the city had chipped at it.

"Sexier than the erotic wall murals and the crowd of naked folks on the upper deck?" Teasing him, she stepped into her shoes.

"You took my fun away."

Gentle yet serious, the comment turned her teasing into something darker. Blind to the rules, she oughn't play this game, but…

"I could give you something else." As she spoke, her fingers curled against the hem of her dress. The fabric rose, tickling her skin as it revealed her, slow inch by slow inch. At the tops of her thighs, the journey ended and she held the dress tight against her crotch.

What am I doing?

If she was going to show her goods to a stranger, why hadn't she done it in a designated, controlled environment on the upper deck?

In the middle of a busy hall, and for a man whose face she couldn't see, she was dragging the dress up farther and revolving in a circle.

"Black panties," he said.

"Yes. Basic, boring—"

"Classic." Still, he stood as if frozen solid, except… Was there tension at the front of his jeans that hadn't been there a few minutes ago? "Now take them off."

"Off?"

"Off. Are you going to give me that, too?"

Feverish, throat tight, fingers jittery, Ona tried to think…tried to breathe…tried to make herself back away from this. Failing, defying herself, she felt the panties scrape along her skin. Glancing down, she saw her ankles loosely bound in the fabric.

She'd literally dropped her panties for a stranger.

"Gonna ask if I like what you're showing me?"

She inhaled in a ragged gulp, touching his fly with her gaze. "If you said you didn't, I'd know you're lying. You're hard. That's all the answer I need."

"Put down your dress now."

"More than you can handle," she diagnosed, yanking the underwear up.

"Wrong about that, 'cause I do want to see more, but not from behind glass."

"You didn't answer the question," she countered, instead of dropping the dress as he'd asked and going about her afternoon as she should.

"From panties down you're much sexier than the erotic art." Now he moved, in easy, sure steps to the side, and Ona decided she would let him come to her. Facing the tower, she waited, listening to his Boston baritone grow closer and more intimate with each word. "Can't say much about the naked folks on the upper deck, seeing as I'm more of a lower deck kind of man."

"I'm a lower deck kind of woman." She let the dress go, and as the hem brushed her knees, she turned her back to the glass tower and her breath caught.

Seven days for seven capital sins, she thought again. Today's sin was most definitely lust.

In a practical sense, he wasn't handsome. It was easy, euphoric to look at a handsome man. But this guy... There was coldness, meanness in his energy, in his stance, but if it was meant to scare her away, it failed. It was what she couldn't identify that drew her. Ona felt nervous, as if she'd been shoved, yet he hadn't touched her.

He had a sexiness that struck without warning or remorse—and a granite-solid body that probably did the same. His height made her feel extremely aware of her shortness—which was crazy, since no one would accuse her of being short. At six-one, she had to limit herself to four-inch heels to avoid feeling like a fairy-tale giant.

The finer points of his attractiveness fell into place fast. The silky-looking dark blond hair was cut short, but there was plenty to twist around her fingers if the urge struck. The arrogant chin and hard, whiskered jaw hinted at harshness she wasn't bucking for. His silver-blue eyes were quicksand, selfishly taking her down deep.

Would it be fair to call him dangerous? Would it be a mistake to call him safe? If he were equal parts good and bad, would it be too risky to straddle him, taking on the good and the bad? Her sense of perception was weak, and unable to judge him, she couldn't decide which she wanted him to be. Breathlessly, brokenly turned on, she did want him inside her while she made up her mind. And she was okay with that.

Look who's on the fast track to skankdom. First you flash yourself, now you can't stop staring. Ah, yes, a functioning brain, just in time to save her from herself.

Taking a chance meant charming her high school crush, not surrendering to lust at first sight with the first stranger to call her feet the sexiest things he'd seen on a multimillion-dollar luxury ship.

A stranger didn't fit into her plans. Matty did, but he was gone and she was on her own. Still on her own. No support system had commiserated with her when she'd second-guessed her snap decision to give up the stage to nurse a man's insecurities. There had been no one to love her through the despair of finding herself out of an ad exec job because of a duplicitous coworker who was screwing her by night and screwing her over by day.

"I felt protected when this tower was between us."

"Now that it's not?" he challenged, his silver-blue perusal scraping across her face and down the trail of buttons on her dress. "What are you feeling?"

Exposed. Lost. *And no, a virtual map can't help me find my way.* Ona brushed a finger over her bangs, motioned to tap her glasses, but she wasn't wearing any. Not the sunglasses, nor the retro midnight-blue-framed eyeglasses she normally wore. Contact lenses were her saviors, rescuing her from colliding with an erotic mural or playing out a number of other klutz fails. "Uh," she stammered, and losing eye contact, she lost ground. Stumbling while standing totally still, she flailed for a moment before regaining her balance.

Was this *flustered*? She didn't do flustered. If only he would stop staring as if he could carve through her facade and see her dirtiest truths, she could get herself together. "I should…" She flapped a hand at the screen. "You probably have somewhere to be."

Bestowing on her a Boston "Yeah" that licked parts of her anatomy long overdue for a nice, thorough licking, the man took off in a gunslinger's stride down the hall in his blue jeans and dark green T-shirt, and Ona had no shame in leaning past the glass tower to study his ass until a line of shipboard crew cut off her view.

Confronting the virtual guide again and its 3D animation and pleasant, sensual audio track, she identified the Sirens' Song Lounge and murmured, "I'm point A. Sirens' Song is point B. Connect us, or else I'll ignore all technology for the duration of this trip."

Futile words. Unplugging wasn't an option for the reunion coordinator, particularly when she was responsible for her group vacationing on an erotic ship. Her smartphone might've vibrated her into a coma had she not Do-Not-Disturbed it after stepping on board. When she did take a moment to deal with it, she'd no doubt find her voice mail filled with her classmates' demands.

Retracting her threat to the guide, she hurried to catch one of the crew members before they turned in unison toward a pair of double doors marked Staff Only and asked for the quickest route to Sirens' Song, traveling by stilettos.

Vanity took a backseat as she passed a corridor announcing gentlemen's and ladies' rest suites. Hanging in a smooth sheet partway down her back, her flatironed hair had fought the good fight against the New York drizzle and Miami humidity, but not even her sultry Carnal Rush gloss could survive her neurotic nibbling habit. Her lips, the inside of her cheek—they weren't safe from her busy teeth.

A drink in Sirens' Song, a few minutes to orient herself with her stateroom, and then Ona would be in full reunion coordinator mode. Well, full reunion-coordinator-slash-sly-seductress mode.

At an unexpected disadvantage, she'd need to brew their chemistry fast to connect with Nicholas before an upper deck kind of woman jonesing for a cruise fix outdrew her.

Ona gave herself to Sirens' Song, gawking at the leather stools, mirrored bar and pops of soft gold and electric pink light spearing through the darkened lounge. Jazzy music rang out from corner to corner. The waitresses in cocktail dresses and tiaras and waiters in suits and ties looked as though they'd been collected from a fashion magazine and given blinged-out staff pins. Bodies clogged the dance floor, traced the bar and scissored through the air on fancy black swings.

She counted four swings with strands of ribbon trailing from the seats. The woman swinging gracefully above Ona held on with one hand and blew confetti from the other.

Specks rained down on Ona and, plucking them from her hair, she gasped at what she held. Money. Crinkled bits of actual US bills.

Touch-screen virtual maps were impressive and crystal staircases splendid, but Ona encountered a hard stop at needlessly destroying money. There'd never seemed to be enough of it in the Tracy household when she'd been a kid. Though her parents had become "nouveau riche" when Ona was in high school, they'd been pissed at her decision to drop out of Juilliard and she'd been made to fund her own survival.

Ona was no finance guru, but shredding money for confetti was mindlessly wasteful. She couldn't justify doing such a thing, couldn't imagine enjoying a drink as others committed what was sacrilege for a Fishtown Philly girl like her.

Deciding to skip the drink altogether, she began to squeeze out of the lounge, but a waitress materialized in front of her.

"Ona Tracy, with the reunion group?"

Ona nodded slowly. "That's me."

"First, welcome. Guest Services asked us to keep an eye out for you and offer a drink of our newest acquisition. Join me at the bar."

Confused—since the guest services manager had taken zero responsibility for the reservations mix-up and had been completely inflexible—Ona figured a decent gesture was better late than never. "Thanks." She glanced from the ceiling to the bar, where it was standing-room only. Seeing that she wouldn't be in the trajectory of shredded cash, she followed the waitress to the mirrored bar and was immediately given a linen napkin.

"A glass of Diamond V, compliments of *The Lure*," the waitress said.

"Diamond V? Interesting name."

"Diamond vodka. We call it that because it's filtered through diamonds. We serve this straight. Are you fine with that?"

"Absolutely. I'm not a lightweight."

The waitress smiled admirably, poured the vodka into a glass tumbler and set it on the napkin. "Shoot, sip, whichever's your preference. It doesn't burn the palate, yet it has excellent impact. Cheers."

"Cheers." Ona decided to shoot, and found the drink pleasantly smooth and shockingly perfect. Could diamond-filtered vodka be anything but perfection? It was almost too luxurious for her taste buds.

What kind of world was this?

After the waitress topped off the glass, Ona started to sip, wanting to savor what must be one of the most expensive drinks to pass her lips. But when her gaze snagged on the stranger from the hallway sitting on a leather stool like a human gargoyle, she almost dropped the damn tumbler.

A wave of vodka splashed her chin, cruised down her cleavage and sank into her dress.

"Oh!" The waitress tossed another few napkins across the bar. "Diamond V's fab and all, but it's not exactly a fashion accessory."

Ona laughed. "Clumsy fingers."

"Call up the shipboard laundry. There's a directory in every cabin. They'll pick up and deliver, and they do excellent work."

Dabbing at the mess, Ona drank what was left in

the glass and approached the man. "I… I don't usually do that."

"Splash alcohol on yourself?"

"Actually, that's happened before." Her throat suddenly went dry, parched as if she hadn't just swallowed down vodka that was likely six figures a bottle. Casually he got off the stool, and though common sense insisted he'd only wrinkle her plans to seduce Nicholas, she took his offer. "I was referencing the, uh, the show-and-tell at the tower. Am I going to be getting a visit from an angry girlfriend?"

"No."

"As in, you're single? As in, you do have a girlfriend but she's okay with sharing?"

"I'm single."

"I thought you had someplace to be."

"Yeah. In front of a cold beer." He turned up a bottle of MGD, and she was pretty certain his Adam's apple hit on her.

"Me, too. I mean, not a beer, per se, but I was looking to have a drink away from the nudie deck." She hesitated. The plan was to take a chance on seducing Nicholas Callaghan, not take a chance on striking up a conversation with a guy who knew what color panties she had on but didn't know her name.

"This place's out of your realm."

"Quite an assumption from someone who doesn't know me."

"Know you, as in the standard stuff? Age, name, how many siblings you have, why you're on this ship, how important you are to have this place pouring you complimentary drinks to spill all over yourself?" He set down the beer, leaned forward and put his hands on the edge of the bar on either side of her, boxing her in. "I can understand you without knowing you. Prefer it, even."

"Well, I don't understand or know you."

"Which do you want?"

"Both."

He chuckled. Sexiest. Grin. Ever.

"I'm Riker Ewan. Thirty-three, ex-marine, no siblings, I was supposed to meet up with somebody, but she didn't show, and I'm not the kind of clientele that gets catered diamond vodka."

A jobless wannabe event planner wasn't that kind of clientele, either, but she said, "Ex-marine at thirty-three? What did it?"

"MARSOC recon job."

"Where?"

"Afghanistan. Picture-pretty blue afternoon—missile attack. Got a nasty scar from pit to hip. Lucky my arm didn't get grinded into Hamburger Helper."

"And in other disturbing visuals…"

"So," he said lazily, "why're you still on my stool?"

"Scars don't spook me." She had one of her own, one she faced every time she took off her bra. "Oh, and anyone who protects and serves our country deserves a free drink now and then."

"I don't need free drinks. Just glad to have a break from fixing drinks. I'm getting my hands dirty in the family business. Pouring folks what they want, wiping the bar, getting in the middle of brawls. Dad's got a place up in—"

"Boston?" she guessed.

"Yeah."

"Accent gave you away. It was one of the first things I noticed about you." Along with his strong-looking legs and, of course, his package.

So he was a bartender. A veteran who worked at his father's place. An average guy with Boston roots and good old-fashioned appreciation for cold beer.

Did he jog familiar neighborhood streets for exercise? Did he lock up the bar, count the register and work on the books 'til sunrise? Did he flirt for his tips, hook up with patrons? Did he care about sports cars and private jets?

Ona pegged him as an old-neighborhood kind of man—stable in the easy-does-it, work hard, raise some hell, sleep, repeat kind of way. She'd grown up surrounded by men like that, and it made him sort of familiar.

"The 'clientele' you mentioned?" she said. "That's not me. Guest Services ordered that drink for me, and I can imagine the only reason why is because management feels sorry for me."

Riker's brows lowered over his eyes, and in the eerie gold and pink light passing through the shadows, it was even more difficult to identify his emotions. "Why?"

"I successfully screwed up my high school's glee club reunion."

"Glee club?"

"Oh, that's funny?" Ona jutted out her chin, and if he touched it she might clock him. "At PAAC, usually the ones who mocked the club were the ones who didn't make the cut and the jocks." Sizing him up, she said, "Football player?"

"Baseball. But athletes and artists can get along okay."

"Not at PAAC. The athletics department went all Pac-Man on the arts department and the glee club was cut right after I graduated."

Riker grunted. "Well, now, I can see where that'd

rain piss on your sunny day. I haven't swung a bat in years, so does that redeem me?"

"Partially." She offered a hand. "Ona Tracy. Twenty-eight, former triple threat, no siblings, and I accidentally booked an erotic ship for a private school's glee club reunion."

"Triple threat?"

"Act, dance, sing. I'm from Philadelphia, but after graduation I tried to float in London, then settled in New York."

"You perform?"

"Not since I passed up *Chicago*." She sighed. "Aside from this reunion, I'm not really in touch with that world anymore. Or this one. Shredded money doesn't fall from the sky where I come from."

"The private school—"

"Is one I attended on a scholarship for low-income students. I'm a talented mezzo-soprano, but depending on which close-minded folks you ask, I'm from the wrong side of Philly. Believe me, the Tracys were more like the Evanses than the Huxtables." She shook her head. "And you probably have no friggin' idea what I'm talking about. I reference classic TV sometimes. It's a quirk. When I get nervous, the quirks come out."

"Ona…" Again with that yummy smile that, under more ideal circumstances, was likely to get her naked in sixty seconds flat. "I get the references. I've seen *Good Times* and *The Cosby Show*. I grew up on reruns."

So this is how you understand me. Because you're like me—the genuine *me.*

"What's making you nervous?" he asked.

"This ship. You."

"'Cause I'm too close?"

"You are eating into my personal space, but that's

not it. You're looking at me too closely. Staring. Is that a common marine thing—the hard, disciplined stare?"

"No." Just "no," and he continued to stare at, study and penetrate her with his quiet thoughts.

"Riker, if from panties down I'm sexier than erotic art, then from panties up, with expensive vodka all over my dress, what am I?"

Appearing to consider this, Riker pushed off the bar. He straightened to a tall statue of a man who did ruthlessly sexy things to an average green shirt. Grasping both sides of her dress's wet open collar, he finally eased his stare from her face to her chest.

Instinctively, Ona clamped her hands on to his solid forearms and fine, dark blond hairs teased her palms. She felt his tendons flex as he freed a button and revealed the lace edge of her basic, boring, classic black bra.

"You're going to strip me in front of everyone in this lounge?"

Those serious blue eyes pinned her puzzled brown ones as the next button escaped, followed by another. "Are you going to let me?"

Sitting on a stool, vodka on her boobs, dress half-open, she wavered long enough to draw his laughter. "Hey, I was deciding."

"All right, okay. But, Ona, look—" Riker skimmed the dress from the collar to where it gaped open at her breasts, touching her where he had absolutely no right to touch her "—in the time it took you to decide, I could've had your clothes on the floor and my hands on your breasts."

"Is that supposed to mean you work fast? Because I'm wondering what else you accomplish with such lightning-quick speed, and I gotta tell you, it's concerning."

"Keep wondering. Or I can show you. I'm at your service."

Was she on fire with temptation? Yes. But her strength could resist, abstain. To leap from a stranger's bed to Nicholas's wasn't a note from her playbook.

"Ooohhh, no. Button me up, marine."

"Okay. And, Ona—from panties up, you're incredible."

Momentarily speechless, she just watched him from underneath her eyelashes as he started to slowly close her dress. At last she managed, "It's not you, Riker. It's not me, either, really. It's Nick. Nicholas Callaghan."

He paused, searching her eyes. "Nick Callaghan, huh? Am I going to be getting a visit from an angry boyfriend?" he said, throwing her earlier question back at her.

"No. No." Ona really ought to let his arms go, except his body fascinated hers. Thick bones. Taut muscle. Warm skin. "I had the hots for him in high school."

"What's 'hots' for a high school kid?"

"I fantasized about him."

Riker's fingers tripped over a button and slid into her pushed-up cleavage. "Uh—"

"Mmm-hmm. But the crush stayed a crush, and I was thinking of changing that during reunion. But I hit a few complications."

"He's got a girl? Gay?"

"I don't know if someone like him sees someone like me as his type."

"Type?"

"How can I put this in a gentle way?" A PC way, even?

"Ona, I grew up with a tough-love dad, spent the

better part of a decade in the marines, and I toss idiots out of a bar just about every night. I don't know what 'gentle' is." He fastened the second-to-top button on her dress, and she was decent again. "Say it. Get it over with. Rip it, like a Band-Aid."

"I don't know if Nick does black."

Riker frowned. "If there's doubt, why the hell would you want to go after a bastard like that? Screw him."

"That's unfair, Riker."

"*I'm* being unfair?"

"Yes, actually. He's a pure-hearted guy—a freakin' saint. If black women or tall women or round-assed women aren't his preference, that doesn't make him a bastard. And I said I don't know if that's the case. In high school he dated blondes and redheads, but if we're talking facts, PAAC—oh, that's the Philadelphia Academy of Arts and Culture—was predominately white. It's diversified over the past decade, but…"

"Ona?"

"What?"

"As a man who *does* do black, I'm going to tell you something. I want to kiss your brown skin, suck your dark nipples into my mouth. I don't care if you're in tall shoes, as long as the rest of you's naked for me. I want to get my hands on that round ass of yours."

"Oh…" Ona gulped for something—a sip of a drink, air, a taste of his filthy mouth. "That was either perverted or poetry."

"It was the truth. So swear to me, if he can't appreciate a smokin' black woman, move on. Find someone else to fantasize about."

Already done—and damn you for being the one.

She wasn't ready to give up on Nicholas for a stranger from Boston. But right now, her attraction to Riker was the most genuine thing about her. She'd come to Miami padded with lies because owning the truth about her life was as harsh as hitting the floor.

A peal of cheers resonated as more handfuls of cash confetti showered the dance floor.

"Gotta say I really friggin' hate that. There's luxury, then there's carelessness." Restraint seemed to seal off his emotions then, and he shrugged a pair of wide shoulders. "Forget it. I just value a buck."

"So do I!" Ona swept her hands up and down his forearms, smiling because, thank God, here was someone she could talk to.

She could flirt with Nicholas, reminisce about glee club and PAAC with the others, but she couldn't truly talk to anyone she'd brought to this ship.

Riker's face neared hers. "Keep stroking me like that, and you're gonna get me hot real fast, Philly."

The smile opened to a head-back, mouth-open laugh. "Shut up, Boston." But she released him, sobering. "My best friend from high school and I planned the craziest scheme. He was going to pretend to be my man, to see if Nick would get jealous."

"Where's the friend?"

"Dead." Ona's teeth caught a chunk of the inside of her cheek. "Matty died over a week ago, but no one told me until I showed up on the pier."

"Hell."

"Yes, exactly. I want to be angry with the ones who are here. I resent that no one cared enough to let me know. But Matty and I lost contact after graduation, and that's his fault and it's mine—not theirs." She shook her head. "I haven't cried for him. Maybe I don't deserve to."

"You respected him?"

"Very much."

"Grief doesn't always show up to the party dressed as tears. But you deserve to mourn your friend. Cross over this."

"A former marine, current bartender and a therapist? The woman who stood you up should be kicking herself—hard."

The closed-off stare made its return. "Just paying forward some advice given to me after my last deployment."

Ona battled the urge to pry, to take down another layer and get even closer. Nicholas was the man she'd shown up on the pier hoping to get closer to, not a stranger who'd understood her before getting to know her and who, in no uncertain terms, wanted to get her naked.

"Thanks, Riker." She stood, brushing against him, involuntarily heating at the contact. "I'd better take a look at my stateroom and get this dress to the dry cleaner."

"Okay." Riker signaled for another beer. "If Saint Nick's the good guy you believe he is, and you're thinking about going ahead with that plan to get him jealous, I can take care of that for you."

"Serious?"

"I don't know how to be anything but."

"Riker…"

Confetti pelted her and, taking it as a warning sign, she began to scoot toward the exit. "I can't have you sacrifice your vacation, so no."

"Being with you ain't a sacrifice, Philly." Swinging up the fresh beer, he saluted her. "Like I said, I'm at your service."

Chapter 3

I'm such a bastard.

Riker Ewan barely registered the smooth force of his frosty MGD. Sexual demand had crashed his system. Then a shot of guilt. Now he was too numb to savor the characteristics of a simple beer.

One of the military's elite, a member of MARSOC, he'd been trained to weather the unpredictable, welcome the dangerous, outmaneuver the impossible.

But the US Marines didn't see Ona Tracy coming. Even skimming six-something barefoot and a walking hazard, she'd captured him in a sneak attack.

The woman wasn't letting herself mourn the loss of the friend she'd asked to help make some dense prick jealous—and he was keeping a beer company, feeling guilty because he'd lied to her?

What was it about her that did him in?

Was it the carefreeness of her springing from foot to

foot at the glass tower as the silvery-pink color on her toenails shimmered? Was it the naughtiness of her pulling down her underwear for him and then letting him work open her dress right here in Sirens' Song? Was it that she was the clumsiest, oddest, realest woman he'd ever ached to get his hands on?

Again, guilt bloomed. He took a harsh swig of beer, resenting emotions he'd fought like hell to store in a vault. The vault kept him calm, easy, alert.

As for Ona… Any of his comrades would've categorized her as a 10 and closed the case.

Riker's brain and body and everything in between groaned yes. Forget skin that looked like smooth, pale chocolate and was guaranteed to taste even better? Erase the slam of heat he'd felt when she'd first set her wide-eyed gaze on him? Pretend the note of naïveté that amplified every sexy, dirty thing about her hadn't already killed him a thousand times over?

This ship wasn't an ark, and Riker hadn't infiltrated *The Lure* to get a soul mate. If he had the sense God gave him, he'd force himself to forget Ona and his crazy-ass offer to step in for her friend.

Fake a relationship—yes, he could do that for her. Ona's sweet vulgarity disqualified her for cute, but he preferred his women funny and frank, and being her man wouldn't be a hardship. But to step aside for some guy who was ignorant to her offbeat sexiness?

The idea of it had him tightening his fist around the beer bottle until he finally took his hand away before the glass could fragment.

"Good deeds ain't on my agenda." The hoarse growl of words was lost in random voices and jazzy music. Giving up the MGD, he shook off the light cascade of confetti and left Sirens' Song.

A series of mistakes had brought Riker and Ona together on a ship where neither of them belonged. Sort of an act of fate, if he had the mind to go for ideas about luck and soul mates and everything else Marisol had sobbed about when she'd walked out two years ago.

Quiet night—one of those sweaty, airless Boston summer nights. Marisol had suggested pot roast and potatoes for dinner; he'd countered with sandwiches and Italian ice at the deli a few streets over, and she'd wiggled off her engagement ring and put it in his palm.

A diamond—one she'd picked from a jeweler's front window. Princess cut, 'cause Marisol had made herself out to be a princess settling for a blue-collar ex-marine.

We don't mesh. She'd entwined her fingers with his. *This doesn't feel right—you know it doesn't. We can't even conceive. It's fate, Riker. Fate says we're not right.*

Whether or not fate told her it was okay to marry someone else, move to California and crank out a pair of babies, Riker didn't know. But she was happy, sent a Christmas card to Dad's bar every year, and he was okay with that.

Fate did right by Marisol, because she was better off in California with her kids and a man who worshipped her. Riker had offered her love and lies. Maybe Marisol carried his love with her, because now all he had left were lies.

Or lies were all he'd had to begin with.

And the legit reason he'd interrupted his stable routine in Boston, left Pint's in Emory Ewan's hands and had boarded this ship was one he wasn't proud of.

Paring down his mother's assets wasn't something he'd swung out of bed and decided to do, but Kate Russ had called his bluff and pissed him off when she'd left him high and dry at Stewart-Russ Cruise Line's head-quarters.

So, yeah, what he'd told the smokin' klutz from Philadelphia about the no-show woman he'd been geared up to meet with was true—in a hazy, technical, slick way.

Only Kate, Emory, a congregation of expensive attorneys and Riker knew the truth. Once shipping magnate heiress Kate Russ's mind bounced off its axis, her secrets had begun to escape.

She'd named him power of attorney.

She'd made him star of her will.

The other secrets Riker didn't want to confront. Not now.

Riker and Kate were connected only by biology and money. Accepting the estrangement, he'd stayed out of her way until her legal group had coerced them to agree to a face-to-face meeting in Miami. Yet she'd escaped him by jetting off to some foreign resort town.

Now he was ready to cut his losses, ease his burdens and show Kate that the son she'd repeatedly rejected but assumed she could trust above all others was a man you didn't want to cross.

John Alison Stewart, her father's friend, might have his name tied to the company, but decades ago Kate had assumed sole ownership. Quiet as kept, Riker owned his father's bar, and had more interest in lying on a bed of hot coals than managing a damn cruise line.

Especially this ship.

Erotic-themed ships with every wild luxury from private butlers to champagne-filled pools to confetti made of shredded one-hundred-dollar bills weren't his style, and *The Lure* would be the first to feel the axe.

Kate had dodged him, likely predicted he'd be running on home to his blue-collar bar—so he bent it to his advantage. Without her in his way, he'd gotten himself a cabin on *The Lure* and knew what he'd do. Gather intel. Strengthen his case. Show his mother that not only had she made a mistake in ignoring him all his life, but she'd been dead-wrong to set her company in his hands.

Expression closed, stride relaxed, Riker wandered the lower level. He had no real destination. The crowds had thickened, and among them a fleet of Pennsylvania private school brats. God help 'em—they'd be turned out before the ship reached the Bahamas.

Even Ona had a war raging between her inhibitions and her inner freak. So nervous. So awkward. Yet in this very hallway she'd shown off her butt and had watched him open her dress in Sirens' Song.

All right, so Riker wouldn't pursue her. But if she came to him ready and eager, he'd take her any way she let him.

As he passed two women, his instincts sharpened. The tiara one of them wore jogged his memory, and he recognized her from the bar. She'd served Ona vodka.

Riker edged toward a water feature that spit streams resembling the double helix. Vigilant, he listened.

"…an impressive drink." Pausing, the waitress waited for passersby to move along. "Raved. She positively raved about it, oh, until she, uh, sort of dumped it on her dress—"

"Oh, damn—"

"No, no, it's fine. A refill and a referral to dry cleaning, and she was good. It was her mistake."

"This time." The other woman, wearing a silver guest services badge, did a discreet 360-degree turn. "Okay, we need to keep the courtesies coming."

"What about the others in her group?"

"Of course we'll accommodate any extras their gratuities can afford, but don't worry too much about them. Ms. Tracy's assumed responsibility, and we won't take that away from her."

"Accounting will go crazy."

"Guest Services can work out a way to explain the expenditures. The managers are having a meeting tomorrow, early am. Until further word, the staff should strive to satisfy Ms. Tracy."

The waitress snorted. "Isn't this level of damage control extreme? A negative review on a travel site's hardly a blemish. It'd be buried in all those religious zealots' complaints that this ship's a prostitution hotspot."

"Ona Tracy's complaint would matter."

"How? She's not high-profile—doesn't know which end's up on a glass of Diamond V."

"The school footing the bill is high-profile. Important people grease that place's wheels. As a cohesive unit, our staff can satisfy Ms. Tracy. Satisfy her, and we see the following results—she won't be digging for answers, Stewart-Russ won't have some private school on its ass, and our employees stay employed. Keep her busy, keep her happy and management's hands are clean."

"Too bad for her. All those people blaming her?"

"Yes, too bad *for her.*"

"Point taken."

"Good. So, I hear there'll be dancing on the crew deck tonight…"

Riker eased around the border of the fountain, and striding away he brought Ona Tracy's predicament into laser-sharp focus.

Keep the courtesies coming. She won't be digging for answers.

Well.

Ona hadn't messed up her classmates' vacation—she'd just been made to believe she had.

Mismanagement of Stewart-Russ Cruise Line's eight-figure ship? Setting up a nice private school babe to take the blame?

Okay, Ona Tracy wasn't *that* nice—thank the sweet Lord. But Stewart-Russ's incompetence was the reason her glee club buddies were on a sex-themed ship. The error had made his mission easier than a ten-dollar hooker, but as he saw things, he had two choices.

Concentrate on his agenda and watch her catch hell she didn't deserve.

Or make it right.

The next day, loneliness made Ona feel claustrophobic in her perfectly bright, spacious stateroom. The cabin had a formal living area, a balcony, marble floors, a minibar and kisses of Greek-influenced decor throughout. There was premium porn accessible on each of the two flat-screen televisions, content she'd innocently stumbled upon while channel browsing for a music station to cheer her on as she heat-straightened her curly hair back into submission. Still she felt tense.

Part of her was hungry for another hit of Riker Ewan's company, but that wasn't the reason she needed to find him.

She had a message for him. He was wrong about her. *Cross over this,* he'd said. *You deserve to mourn your friend.*

Ona didn't deserve to mourn Matty. She'd been a lousy friend while he was alive, and was an awful grieving friend now.

Yesterday, after changing out of the vodka-soaked dress and playing Miss Do-It-All for her classmates, she'd thought she could cry. She had set the high school yearbook she'd brought along and a box of Kleenex tissues on the bed, sat down with her smartphone and tapped in keywords from *Matthew Grillo obituary Juneau* to *Alaska bush pilot dead*, finding news stories describing his plane crash.

But she hadn't cried. Not a tear. The mental games she relied on to trigger emotions for the stage had rendered no results. Feeling cold, she'd tucked away the yearbook and tissues, put on her tightest dress over her raciest lingerie and spent a late night in a VIP room of the ship's casino, swallowing shots and trying to earn Nicholas Callaghan's attention.

When she'd been just tipsy enough to consider inviting Nicholas to her cabin, because maybe—just maybe—he wouldn't degrade her in private the way he unconsciously had in front of the others, she caught herself and returned to her room alone.

Make that a lousy friend *and* a sorry excuse for a seductress. Any competent actor could pretend to cry or flirt. It sickened her more than her early-morning hangover to fake grief over someone she genuinely loved and lost. And after what Riker Ewan had said in Sirens' Song yesterday, she was beginning to resent that she had to earn Nicholas's attention.

Casual looks over blackjack and craps tables weren't rewards. A stroke down her hair as he pressed behind her and helped her yank an old-timey slot machine arm wasn't a declaration of desire. Pulling her onto his lap while he drank liquor, played his poker hand and cavalierly ignored her conversation was hurtful.

As some unspoken rule of last night, she was the only woman welcome at Nicholas's table, and her role was to sit—not speak. Anyone who'd noticed Ona decorating his lap and that he scarcely acknowledged her hadn't said anything aloud, and somehow that made Ona regret what she was chasing.

Ona Tracy, Nicholas Callaghan's personal skeeze. If it were true, then she could manage the sting of it. But the reality was she'd absorb the whispers and shaming looks but would have none of the advantages of being linked to him. At the casino Nicholas hadn't seen Ona, not actually. No stares, no smiles, no gesture to assure that he saw her as more than an object in a skintight dress to keep his lap warm while he spent more money on liquor than he won in cards. Ona hankered for something concrete, something she could trust. She wanted to be seen, heard, understood. And yes, damn it, she wanted to be wanted.

Day two of their cruise was half over, and all she'd learned was that Nicholas couldn't gamble his way out of a paper bag. It was sort of endearing, the way he accepted his high-dollar-amount losses with laughter and mock threats to the others.

Scrolling back to last night, as she lazed on her cabin's balcony and dined on a typical I-drank-too-much-the-night-before-now-I-need-carbs brunch of French toast, scrambled eggs, bacon and a whipped-cream-topped fruit medley, Ona supposed she was overly sensitive to how no one had reflected on the sad fact that one of their own was gone.

There was an empty space where Matty should be. At least, in Ona's heart there was. Last night she'd filled that hole in the worst way—drinking a series of shots she didn't remember and allowing a man she admired to treat her in a way that made her uncomfortable with herself.

Peculiar thing was, she realized as she wrapped a

chunk of French toast around a spear of cantaloupe, she'd been even bolder and bawdier with Riker but hadn't come away with heavy regrets.

With Riker, an average guy who paid the bills with bartending tips and had some nasty scars under his average-guy clothes, she'd felt daring and naughty. With Nicholas, a man of prestige and privilege and power, she'd felt scuzzy and sleazy. For Riker, she'd bared her body. For Nicholas, she'd sat on his lap and held his glass as he gambled volumes of cash while he talked investments.

She didn't know Riker…so why did Nicholas seem like a stranger?

"Stop, Ona," she said over the rush of propellers and ocean beyond her balcony, picking up a strip of bacon. "Big girls stick to their plans. Taking a chance on Nick is the plan."

She bit into the crispy perfection as a knock reverberated out the open balcony doors to her table-for-one. Bacon in hand, she hurried inside and opened the door to the last person she expected to see.

"Regan Waltz. How did you find my room?" Damn it. "I mean, what can I do for you?"

"You wear glasses?"

"Guilty," Ona said slowly, touching the frames.

Regan's amber gaze peered over the tops of tortoise sunglasses and moved to Ona's hand. "Bacon? You're eating greasy, fattening, artery-clogging bacon?"

Ona chomped into it. "I *was* eating it. But since you said all that, I think I might make love to it."

"I meant no offense, Ona." Regan swayed in her flimsy baby-doll cover-up, turning halfway to reveal sandals that boasted six-inch diamond heels. "It's just that, for your welfare, I'm thinking that someone with your physique shouldn't be such a fatty-food junkie. If you were careful, you might not feel the necessity to hide in your cabin while everyone else is on the deck."

"Which deck?"

"The lower one. I refuse to try the upper deck. I'm liable to sit on a chaise and end up pregnant."

Ona smirked. "Was that your attempt at a joke, Regan?"

The woman's mouth began to soften, but she jerked back as though catching herself before she tumbled off the edge of a cliff. "The predicament you put PAAC and your classmates in isn't a joke. I bought disinfectant and hand sanitizer to protect myself."

Chewing, Ona leaned against the doorjamb. "If you're looking to protect yourself from getting pregnant on this ship, you're going to need more than disinfectant and hand sanitizer. Might I suggest something latex?"

"You don't get it, do you, Ona? This isn't a laughing matter. Nothing good can come out of this vacation and you're to blame. Single-handedly, you're damaging our school's reputation as well as mine."

"PAAC won't be singing my praises, I'm already prepared for that." She wasn't, but she hoped she would be. "You're a grown woman and have a right to engage in any consensual and legal act you'd like to on this ship. That includes eating copious amounts of crispy bacon."

"Oh? Does it also include going to a sex machine demonstration?"

"A what?"

"You heard me! Jane Charley and I had a shopping date this morning but she blew me off, and I found out the reason why. There's a sex machine in one of those roped-off VIP rooms and this morning people were invited in for a demonstration."

"I'm sorry—a what? I'm thinking of a James Brown song."

"Perhaps all the bacon fat's going to your brain." Regan took the last chunk from Ona's hand and ate it, and she looked to be enjoying it a little too much. "A sex machine is an actual mechanical thingamajig. I asked a ship staff member, and let's simply say that the words *dildo* and *nipple shocks* didn't leave many blanks to fill in. And Jane Charley was there."

Jane was only member of the club Ona had run into after graduation. They'd both been Equity, participating in an actors' studio workshop in New York, and had sworn to stay friends. But somewhere between Ona being cast in *Chicago* and bowing out, and Jane snagging the role of Christine in *Phantom of the Opera*, which had led her to making an opera house her home, they'd lost touch.

"Okay," Ona said, shrugging. "So it was thoughtful of Jane to not ask you to come along. Sex machines aren't for everyone, but good for her for finding something that'll probably *really* help her hit that high E."

Regan pushed up her sunglasses. "You've surprised me, Ona."

"How so?"

"Well, you're in rare form with so many, ooh, one-liners for someone who's hiding in her room. Last night at the casino you were…popular." Without asking permission, Regan used her petite size to her advantage, ducking and floating into the cabin. "And the drinks. You certainly drank a lot. I told Jane and the other ladies that if not for Nicholas Callaghan keeping you upright on his lap, you'd drink any of the men under the table."

A moment stretched taut before Ona suspected the hidden insult. "Hey—"

"No offense. Never offense." But the snap of fire in Regan's eyes contradicted her words. "This isn't high school, and besides how your actions reflect on our school, I don't particularly care how you carry yourself. Cole Stanwyck mentioned you're seeing someone on this ship. I thought I'd check up on you, to make sure your man didn't take your old times' sake flirting out of context. Where is he?"

Oh, right. Ona had lied to Cole about being with another man, hadn't she? "We aren't sharing this cabin. He has his own."

"Why?"

"Our relationship's still new, and—" *Keep the lie going strong. You can do it.* "—and, um, we didn't want to get bored with having sex in the same cabin the entire trip."

Regan's lips made a faint smacking sound as her mouth dropped open. "Well, how much sex are you having if you need two cabins to do it in?"

"Plenty," Ona lied. Oh, she was lying so hard. She hadn't had sex in a while, and the closest she'd come was stripping herself because a stranger with a sexy Boston accent and a phenomenal body had told her to. "Sex, sex, sex. It's what we love, me and my...uh... sex man."

"Sex man." Regan blinked. "What's his name?"

Ah, crap, she did have to give this figment of her lies a name. If he was giving her more sex than her cabin could handle, then he deserved a hell of a name. "How about I introduce you to him, later? He can tell you his name himself." All that would do was give her enough time to build her fake sex man and create a compelling reason why neither Regan nor anyone else from PAAC would ever meet him. "Regan, look. I may have gotten us stuck on the wrong ship, but as reunion coordinator I'm committed to seeing to it that the group makes the best of this 'predicament.' You're miserable."

"Precisely. Contrary to the swipe you took at me on the pier yesterday, I no longer use my assets to get things I want. I cleansed, eliminating toxins from all areas of my life. I have moral standards."

"I'm glad you shared that with me. But not everyone's going to adopt your moral standards. We're all different. We agree on some issues, disagree on others. It makes for some cool debate. What I want to know is why you seem so empty. I can see it."

"I'm just tired."

"Spa visits are included in our reservations. Get a facial or a wrap or a rubdown or something. Or consider this. There hundreds of passengers onboard. Mingle. Meet someone. Take a breath and talk."

"Strange, you have some passionate romance cooking but you divert the conversation away from your man."

"This reunion is about PAAC. Not Riker."

Oh, no. Riker wasn't her man. Why had she said that?

"Riker?" said Regan, curious. "All right. I'll look forward to shaking his hand."

"Sorry—no. He can't stand the smell of hand sanitizer." Extraordinarily immature, but how could Ona resist when the woman had swiped her bacon, barged into her cabin and slut-shamed her—the biggest strike being the bacon-swiping? "Never any offense."

Stiffly, Regan went to the door. "If you mean that, change out of those sweatpants and come with me to the pool. Everyone's getting together there to catch up."

"I didn't know everyone had set something up for

the deck." Slightly irked that she'd been clued in at the last minute yet again, Ona almost sighed in frustration. At least someone—Regan Waltz of all people—had included her. The olive branch might be poisonous, but it was a risk she'd take to forge a positive reconnection with her peers and have a chance of picking this reunion up off its butt. The casino hadn't been the ideal venue for everyone to slow down and talk. Poolside conversation might do them all some benefit, and Ona craved knowing what ten years had done to a bunch of private school performers. She'd read everyone's profiles, but to really know what time did to a person, you had to talk to them. "Give me ten and I'll come with."

Exchanging the glasses for contact lenses, and trading the sweats for a black mesh bikini top with a bow and matching bottoms, Ona swept up her swim tote and joined Regan.

"That is not a bikini," Regan accused. "It's sheer."

"Not completely. The bow hides the nipples and the bottoms are solid at the crotch and booty crack."

Scoffing, Regan insisted, "I'm only considering your welfare."

"You said that before."

"Last night you were on Nicholas's lap and now you're going to be lounging around a pool wearing that in front of him? It's an attention-getter."

An attention-getter... Perfect.

They'd gotten no farther than halfway down the hall before Cole Stanwyck nudged between them, securing his arms around their waists. "The two hottest women on board. I would've been the king of PAAC if I had the pair of you keeping my arms full. Where are you headed?"

Ever the composed, cool one, Regan gave her deep

gold curls a toss. "Cole, juvenile come-ons don't affect me."

"That hurts, Regan. Stilts, make it up to me."

Hesitant to linger in his company, Ona at last said, "We're going to the lower deck."

The walk was uneventful, meaning Cole didn't try to stick his hand between her legs, as he'd tried to when they were seniors at PAAC. Ona hadn't realized she was sweating until the three of them arrived at the deck. What further concerned her was that she might've panicked had Regan Waltz not been there to protect her in a strange, accidental way.

"If you're going to be sitting on anybody's lap, let it be mine," Cole said as he escorted Ona and Regan to the doors where two crew members stood by to offer assistance. "Nicholas didn't book you for the entire trip, did he?"

Regan snapped, "Ona has someone, Cole, and it's not Nicholas. She has someone else and they're having plenty of sex. So can you please stop the bullshit?"

Ona and Cole froze as Regan untangled herself from his hold and started to stalk out on the pool deck ahead of them.

"Regan, wait," Ona tried, craning her neck to see the woman through the people cutting across her line of vision.

Regan paused to accept a rolled cool towel and a bowl of fruit from a row of pool refreshment staff. "The only reason I'm not going to a champagne pool right now is because Rajon asked everyone to show up here," she hollered to the pair. "I'm only doing this because I respect that man more than I'll ever respect you, Cole."

"Repressed bitch," he sneered at Regan's back.

Ona pushed against him. "Let me go. I will not listen to you call her that."

"You don't like her, and she sure as hell doesn't like you."

"That's true. I'm not going to deny it. But I didn't come to this deck to make alliances. I came to catch up with the group. Some of us want this to be a positive experience."

Cole snatched his arm from her waist, and because she'd been struggling against him, she stumbled at the abrupt freedom. He made no move to steady her—not that she would've let him, anyway. "I'm positive you've been experiencing Nicholas Callaghan."

"Think what you want," she said, scanning the deck and finding roughly half the group.

"If you're with somebody, where is he?" Cole persisted.

Ona felt sweaty again, uncomfortably hot, but a cool towel or fruit or concoctions from the pool deck's snazzy bar wouldn't be of any relief. Stress sawed at her nerves, and she wanted to get away. "He's…"

"Where, Ona?"

"He's—" Ona's gaze swung across the deck, and he was there. Not a made-up sex man or a man she could have a genuine relationship with, but Riker Ewan. One hand gripped a safety railing, the other held his phone, and taut muscles bulged across his arms and back. A gray T-shirt and athletic shorts today, and his dog tags were out, dangling from a simple silver chain. Sunglasses concealed his eyes, but she recognized him clearly. Her body had sensed his. "He's there, on the phone."

"I don't believe you." Cole said it calmly, as though he almost enjoyed cornering her and forcing her to face her own lies. "Admit you lied and I won't have you embarrass yourself in front of the club."

"Not that I owe you any explanation, Cole," she served back, "but I'm not available, and my marine probably won't appreciate that I've had to tell you so many times. You need to leave me alone."

For effect, she crossed the deck to Riker and took his phone from his hand. Disconnecting the call, she whispered solemnly, "I'm sorry. I'm so sorry, Riker, but I need your help."

A frown immediately creased his face. "It's yours. What's wrong?"

"You told me you're at my service. If you meant what you said yesterday about pretending to be with me, kiss me." Ona wrapped an arm around his shoulders, because she would start trembling if she didn't hold on to something solid. So many men in her life had assumed that just because she was tall, seemed strong, she never needed support. Would Riker give her that?

"Are you sure about this, Ona?"

"Kiss me," she said again. "Make it good. Make it so nothing and no one else on this deck exists."

"Put my phone in my pocket," he said calmly in her ear, his lip moving over the shell. "My hands are going to be on you and I'm not gonna take them off until we're done here. And he's going to envy me. He's going to want to have this chance with you."

Ona nodded because it was true, technically. To be further technical, it was Cole who'd envy Riker and who'd want this chance with her. She didn't know what Nicholas wanted.

Riker took her in stages. Large hands grasped her hips, preparing her. Eyes that were simultaneously blue as ice and gray as smoke perused her. Beautiful, warm, hungry mouth claimed hers with a sudden force that had her head snapping back and her legs collapsing.

His teeth captured her lips one at a time, and his tongue tasted her. To have his strength wrapped around her... To have his firm mouth open to hers...

No one had ever said a kiss could void all sensation but arousal. It was a lesson she had to learn for herself as he held her and grinded. Moving against her like this, he spoke to her, admitted his desire and coaxed her to admit hers.

It didn't feel like a first kiss. It was absent of expectation and curiosity and nervousness. There was just addictive pleasure.

A throat cleared, and Ona finally lifted her mouth from his.

Beside them, Jane Charley stood in a vintage polkadot swimsuit. A dab of Noxzema coated her nose from bridge to turned-up tip. "Sorry to interrupt, but people are staring, and someone just bet someone else that clothes would be coming off within five minutes. Ona, a sec?" Jane took her elbow, guiding her a few steps away, and Riker discreetly turned toward the wall to disguise the unquestionable stiffness she'd felt at the front of his shorts.

"Cole Stanwyck stormed off," Jane said confidentially, her brown eyes alight with intrigue. "I think he's feeling the effects of being such a condescending creep. No woman should spend a vacation obligated to a man like that, so I can understand your predicament. But, Ona, honey, if you had a perfect man stashed on this ship, why'd you lend yourself to Nicholas last night?"

"I didn't lend myself, Jane. Regan and Cole and now you—you're all acting like crazy people, judging a grown woman and a grown man for sitting together in a public casino."

Jane shook her head. "It's not what happened *in* the casino. Regan got fed up with the show you two were putting on and got out of there, but I told her Nicholas left shortly after you did. I wasn't the only one who noticed."

"That may be true, but when I was taking off makeup and wrapping my hair, I'm fairly sure I was by my lonesome."

"Oh. So Nicholas didn't go to you?"

"No, Jane. When it comes to Nicholas, if I'm out of his sight, I'm out of his mind. Sometimes I'm out of his mind when I am in his sight. It's always been that way." Ona looked toward the pool and caught Regan glaring in their direction. "Regan's not happy. According to her, I'm directly responsible for a sex machine corrupting you today. If looks could kill, I'd be dead."

Jane arched a brow. "You're very much alive. We're all lucky to be."

"Oh, my God. Matty. Why did I just say that? Why would I say that?"

"Ona, it's okay."

It wasn't, but she nodded anyway.

"Smile, all right?" Jane said. "Which of us has it worse right now? I'm divorced and my friend's angry because I went to a sex machine demonstration on an erotic ship. You were just kissing the sexiest man I've seen in ages. What is he, army?"

"Marine. Ex."

"Seriously, I'd drink that guy's piss from a cup."

Ona's mouth twisted. "You're on your own for that one. I don't really do much. Piss drinking's under the *don't do* umbrella."

"Open your mind. It won't hurt you."

"Sorry, are we still talking about drinking urine, or have we moved on to opening one's mind?"

"Ona, it's like this. A woman has her limits. Most of these limits she'll find herself pushing for the right person. You'd be surprised to find out what you're willing to do for love. Or a head-to-toe orgasm."

Right person—Riker Ewan? Not at all. They were just… He was only… "Uh, Jane, now you're reminding me of that Meat Loaf song," she said, throwing the conversation toward a babbling tangent to discourage Jane, "and since I still don't know what *that* is, I'm probably going to become fixated on analyzing the lyrics and the video—"

"As much as I'd love to go on that journey with you, Ona, I should get back. They're saving me a spot at the shallow end. All Rajon had to do was ask and the guest services people reserved the entire pool for us. Cocktails are forthcoming. Your man's welcome. A marine. Oooh, so down-to-earth." Jane flaunted a smile brighter than the Noxzema on her nose and flounced to the PAAC gang that had massed at the pool. Detecting Jane harbored information, Regan, in her diamonds and designer swimsuit, navigated the pool as determined and dangerous as a shark, and the two began to whisper-gossip the way they had when they'd ruled the halls in school.

Riker appeared beside her. "I didn't go to my high school reunion, but something's telling me if I had, I wouldn't have seen so many frowning people."

"Guest Services gave us the pool for the afternoon. Free drinks are on the horizon. Still, they're angry to be on this ship."

"I know anger, and this ain't it. Those people aren't angry."

"Then what are they? I spent four years with them and think I'm a decent judge of character, but please, go ahead and tell me what you think they are."

"Calculating. Stressed. Confused. All that's got more to do with real life than it does with the cruise itself."

Was he aware that he'd just described Ona, too? Yesterday she'd made up her mind to put real life on hold for the duration of the trip. She couldn't allow a shabby time at a casino and some silly gossip to burn her resolve. She'd do bold things—even bolder than showing off her fanny—and say what blossomed in her mind. With Riker, she could. He didn't know that among her collection of failures was the only one she'd succeeded in: letting people use her. But he'd said he didn't need to know her to understand her. He accepted her as she was.

"Hey," he said. "You still have my phone."

"Oops." She handed it back and shared her cell number. "Put me in your contacts list. We can talk about old-school TV. Maybe we can search this place for a restaurant that'll make some plain, messy American food and… I don't know…we can share a Philly cheesesteak."

"No."

No? "I… No, it's perfectly okay. I misread this—"

"Hey, Ona? I meant no to sharing a Philly cheesesteak. You don't share a good cheesesteak sandwich. So we're gonna get two."

Ona laughed, stunned at his ability to sink her then bring her back up sky-high again. She needed to steal back her equilibrium. Moving her lips over his, she said, "While I'm catching up with all these calculating, stressed and confused people, you might want to get that tent in your shorts under control."

"I can manage."

"What if I said I wanted to manage it for you?"

"Ona… I thought you had your eye on Saint Nick."

"I did. I still do. I'm not asking for a relationship, Riker. In fact, I was mulling tracking you down to tell you how wrong you were about me deserving to grieve my friend. Truth is, last night I did something I regret and I wasn't feeling good about myself until the bacon and French toast."

"I'm not following you."

"Don't follow. Stay beside me. It'll all make sense in a second. I haven't gotten anywhere with Nicholas. He still looks right through me. There's another man, Cole. He's not the world's most respectful guy. I want him to back off. That's why I came to you and asked you to kiss me."

"Pick the asshole out of the lineup."

"Cole's not out here. Jane said he saw us together and split." She folded her hands over his shoulders. As long as she could touch him, she'd know that she had something strong to count on. "You were here, right here, exactly when I needed you. Meant to be. What is that?"

"I heard somebody call it fate before."

"Fate and I are going to be friends if it's got my back like that." Ona raked down her hair as a surge of wind stirred it. After a few moments of combating the breeze, she gave up the fight. "Why are you watching me?"

As his hands cradled her face, she thought that he might kiss her again. But his fingers moved up to rake her wind-tossed bangs back. "Nice forehead. I want to ask you something. Take it as a stupid guy question or a stupid white guy question if you want, but give me a straight answer. What do you do to it—your hair?"

Ona's eyes bugged. Was that why he'd run his fingers

through it? To see if he'd find tracks? "Did you touch my hair to find out if I'm wearing a weave?"

"No. I touched you because I feel good when I do. The question remains, though. What do you do to it?"

"To get the kink out, you mean? This is the 'ethnic hair talk.' I'm not having the ethnic hair talk with you. No man, except my salon-boyfriend in New York, has come near the ethnic hair talk."

Riker splayed his fingers and slowly dragged his hands through from roots to tips. "No wonder you're not with any of them now. This is how I want to understand you. I want to know what you look like when no one's around to judge you."

Curly haired, bespectacled and usually wearing clothes made from practical cotton. "Riker, that's not part of our arrangement. That kiss was part of the arrangement. Not this discussion."

"It is. That kiss was a sample of how I'd handle you if you were mine. That's what I demand from you. Give me what I give you. Handle me, Ona, 'cause I'm sure as hell gonna handle you. If we're making this look real for them, I want something real from you."

"Are we fighting? I feel that we're fighting."

Stroking her bare back, he kissed her, then he wound the tails of her bikini top's bow around his hand. "I'm challenging you, Ona. Ask yourself when was the last time a man looked at you long enough to decide you were worth challenging, then find me when your mind's made up. Tell me we can be real with each other, or tell me to go to hell. Just make up your mind about it."

When they parted, Ona pressed her hands to her chest, offering protection to her racing heart. As she watched him stride away, her periphery captured a broad-shouldered figure standing a short distance away.

Nicholas. And he was watching her. Really, for the first time, focusing on her.

Ona hesitantly lifted a hand to wave, and when he acknowledged her with a smile, she thought, *I'll be damned. All it takes is a boy playing with a toy to make another boy realize he wants the toy.*

Not again. Not again was she reducing herself for Nicholas Callaghan's benefit. With Riker she was a woman and with Nicholas a toy?

There was history and promise with Nick. With Riker, there was only fantasy that they both knew would burn itself out. It was a flame clinging to a candle's wick. He was Boston, she was Philly.

Funny, that never seemed to matter an iota when they were in each other's vicinity.

"PAAC brats, front and center!" Rajon Sneed called as his wife, Kimora, maneuvered his wheelchair close to the pool and two bartenders bearing serving trays put a brandy cocktail in every hand.

Ona took her drink but stood on the border, part of the group but not totally in the group. She didn't want an in-depth "What have you been up to these past ten years?" conversation, because she wasn't in a mood to lie about not performing on Broadway because she'd grown bored with singing, or lie about not belonging to an advertising firm because she was such a hot commodity that no firm could afford her, or lie about her torrid relationship with an ex-marine.

"Everybody got a glass?" Rajon asked, holding up a bottle of brandy. As the PAAC brats, sans Cole, assembled, other guests sharing the deck had begun to look up from their tablets and pluck out their earbuds. Now they didn't try to mask their curiosity. "All right, I'm pouring one out. For Matthew Grillo."

Touched by his kindness, Ona watched Rajon turn the brandy bottle and splash the exquisite deck. Silence circled the pool, and she felt herself edging closer to the others before she realized what she might do. She closed her eyes. Then a poignant Sinéad O'Connor pop ballad began to fall from her lips.

Her voice sounded small, broken to her own ears, but this wasn't about performance. It was about conveying a message to the others and to herself and to her good friend who wasn't here.

On the third line, a charming feminine voice brought harmony, and Ona opened her eyes to see Jane singing from the shallow end of the pool. On the chorus Regan and a few other women from their class joined, and they sang goodbye.

Nicholas offered his hand to Ona, and taking it she let him help her into the citrus-scented pool.

Riker Ewan was right about grief. It didn't always show up to the party dressed as tears. Sometimes it came in the form of a song.

Chapter 4

Riker left a two-word message on Ona's voice mail that night: *I'm sorry.* He regretted that he'd angered her, not that he'd challenged her, but he kept it brief and blunt and hoped he hadn't just annihilated the best, strangest relationship he'd ever had. So hell no, he hadn't second-guessed going straight to her stateroom when she'd answered him with I want to show you something.

Based on their first electric encounter, which still had him caught up in visceral, perverted dreams, whatever Ona Tracy wanted to show a man was probably worth seeing.

Ona opened her door wearing a baseball T-shirt, glasses and a whole lot of hair. Corkscrews sprang out in every direction, falling past her shoulders.

I like that. I need that.

"You're standing there, looking like that, either 'cause you love me or you hate me."

Laughing, she grasped the bottom of his shirt and

urged him inside. "Hey there. I'm Ona Tracy. I have curly hair, wear glasses and am passionately in love with cotton shirts."

"New York Yankees, Ona? I thought you'd be a Phillies fan."

"Yankees. It's in the blood. Me, my parents, their parents..." Her lashes lowered. "Are you a Red Sox fan?"

"Now and forever."

"Then that puts us on opposites sides of the rivalry. I could take the shirt off."

Riker quit walking. "If I'm in your cabin and you're offering to take off clothes, does that mean we're cool?"

"Yeah. In fact, I asked you here to demonstrate what I do to my hair. You asked and I'm gonna show you. C'mon over to the vanity." She gestured to a spread of bottles and instruments, and he was reminded of the space station his ex-fiancée had kept set up in their bedroom. "Lost yet?"

"It can't be rocket science."

"True. It's worse. It's *hair* science." Ona sat on the vanity. "I've already washed and dried it, so all that's left is heat-protecting and styling."

"You look hot like this."

She gazed at him through the mirror. Smiled. "Thanks. It's that no one's ever— I mean... Forget it." Shaking her hair, she reached for a spray bottle. "Small sections, heat protect, comb and iron it out. Simple but time-consuming, especially when you've got a lot of hair."

"Let me help you."

"If you burn me, I'll never speak to you again." She knit her brows. "Really, I'm scared you'll be too heavy-handed."

"When my ex-fiancée broke her wrist, she had me curl her hair. Straightening can't be all that different."

"You were engaged?"

"Yeah. Marisol. She ended it three years ago."

Ona sectioned off some of her hair and clipped the rest out of the way. "Was it bad? The ending-it part?"

"Tough to get used to her not being there. She's a solid woman. A real broad, you know?" He took the comb and brought it to the ends of her hair. "She was my angel after I left the marines."

"Did she show you how to comb out the ends first?"

"Seems like it'd hurt like hell to be ripping at it from the roots."

"I'm really getting to like you, Riker." She handed him what looked like a pair of tongs. "Flat iron. The plates are hot—watch yourself. No more than three passes, or I'll end up with heat damage. Please don't make me regret this."

Chuckling, Riker straightened the section, and when she seemed satisfied with the results, they kept at it until it was all silky straight. Once she tied it with a strip of silk, she led him to the bedroom and curled up beside him.

"Do you still love Marisol?"

"Yeah," he said. Things had been rough when she left, but he hadn't quit loving her just because he'd fallen out of love with her. "Do you still love any of your exes?"

"Only one. Matty. He was my friend, but I had a lot of firsts with him, so he was more on the borderline between friend and lover." Ona's hand settled over his heart and he held it there. "As for the others, they turned me into a victim. One got me fired from my ad firm. He was leaking our campaign to a competitor and pretty much framed me. Another said he would marry me if I quit the theater. I'd been drifting out of the biz by that point, so I went along with it—and boom, he left me. My college boyfriend was a dancer I tutored. He made the grade, made out with me and when he found a lump on my breast he dumped me."

"What a jerk."

"I had a lumpectomy, and everything turned out okay, but that kind of set the tone for the kinds of guys I'd end up with, huh? Users." Sighing, she turned onto her side, away from him. "Nicholas is already established. He'll look out for me."

"He can't look out for you if he can't even look at you." Slowly straddling her hips, he lost himself in those dark eyes. "I'm looking. I want to look."

Slipping the shirt over her head, she dropped back onto the bed and let him look. The deep brown scar was on her left breast. Interrupting the silence, she said, "We should agree on the details of this fake relationship."

"Right," he said, palming both breasts, watching her eyes for the faintest hint of no. None came, and he lowered to kiss her sternum, lick her areolas, suck her tight nipples. "This fake relationship."

"It's not real," she uttered, her eyes sliding closed as his hand was magnetized to the warm apex of her thighs. "It can't be real."

"I'm just saying we arrive in Nassau in the morning and it seems a senseless waste to travel on an erotic-themed ship and not participate in anything erotic."

The comment triggered all kinds of warning sirens to blare through Ona's instincts. Yesterday they'd dispersed after gathering poolside and honoring Matty with brandy and a capella singing. They hadn't all met up again until this afternoon when Guest Services, which she'd come to decide was a department comprised of darlings, had formally requested that she and her party attend a wine tasting at the ship's most exclusive restaurant. Now they were lulled, aimlessly walking through the ship and, in Jane Charley's case, baiting trouble.

Ona, bringing up the rear with Nicholas, who'd draped his arm around her shoulders, pulled her champagne lollipop from her mouth and chimed in, "Some of us *have* participated in erotic activities."

Such as engaging in extremely heaving petting with Riker Ewan last night...

"On *The Lure*?" Skeptical, Jane wiggled her brows at Ona. "Boudoir photos? Role-playing? Peep shows? Please. You told me yourself you don't do much. I watched a sex machine demonstration and wouldn't mind seeing it again." She suddenly stopped walking. "Ohhh. I let a secret slip, didn't I?"

Ona glanced up at Nicholas. "Jane's drunk." As the others began to jeer and the group started to quarter itself, she was reminded of the night she'd gotten her classmates into a grimy Philadelphia club and some of them had ended up doing blow in a restroom. It was the first night she'd been afraid of where desperation to be liked could lead. Leaving Nicholas, she got in front of everyone. "Okay, let's go about it this way. One person chooses a VIP room and everybody goes in." Noticing Regan Waltz seemed agitated, Ona clarified, "Regan chooses the VIP room."

Complaints roared and someone shouted, "Not her! She wouldn't let us color in a porno coloring book."

"They have those here?" someone else hollered.

Yes, *The Lure* offered erotic coloring books. Ona

knew because she'd bought one as a souvenir to never show her parents. "Regan's choosing our entertainment. C'mon up here, Regan. Find a black velvet rope that's offering something tonight."

Ona returned to her spot in the back of the group and Regan sashayed ahead of everyone else, shaking her head at a pedestal promoting a BDSM training class and pretending to gag at the sex toys seminar. As the others' irritation grew, Ona murmured to Nicholas, "Whatever she chooses, swear you won't tap out without taking me with you."

"Swear." Nicholas gave her shoulders a squeeze. "Don't see your guy around, so I'm going to take care of you."

Inside, part of Ona cheered with pride while another part castigated her for it. It was incredible to feel elevated, superior, untouchable. But it wasn't incredible to feel this way because a man she wanted ten years ago decided to toss her scraps of attention.

Yo, he's a gambler. He doesn't want you. He just wants to beat the other guy.

Ona faltered, gazing at Nicholas to find him eyeing Regan. "Nick—"

"Found one, everyone," Regan sang cheerily. "Massage instruction, and—" she consulted her oversize pink diamond watch "—it starts on the hour, so we should hurry. This one might be useful. I have tension in my neck."

Checking their phones at the door with security and picking up bracelets for reentry, they all shuffled in.

The atmosphere seemed to hug Ona. Scented oils. Sensual R & B music. Amber-colored light caressing a raised platform that featured a wide bed draped with burgundy and cream silk. Oil to aid the glide of skin on skin. Peacock feathers to tease. Stones to rest on pressure points.

As the PAAC group scattered to sit wherever seats remained, Ona let Nicholas draw her through the crowd.

Am I with him? Or am I following him?

Agitated that it mattered, frustrated that she'd chosen now to doubt what she wanted from him and for herself, she forced herself to finish what she'd started with him—and to do it with pride.

Caressing her champagne lollipop with her tongue, Ona leaned close to Nicholas. "There's wine. And dessert."

"Moderation, Ona?"

"Meaning?"

"The eating. The next time you're invited to a tasting, don't sample something simply because it's there." Nicholas's hand traveled down her arm, stopped at her wrist. "Wine, cake, lollipops. I'm saying this for your welfare."

For your welfare...

Where had she heard that before?

"If my appetite turns you off, say so," Ona said. Criticism didn't bruise her feelings—casting directors had called her anything from an Amazon to a fat-ass—but it was the coldness of his aura that had her straightening in her seat.

"It doesn't turn me off," he said quietly. "You're a hot woman, Ona. Calories do ugly things to hot women."

Ten years ago—hell, even two days ago—Ona would've been delighted to her Fifth Avenue–manicured toes to hear Nicholas Callaghan call her *hot*. But the word was so deeply buried under his hideous words and sexist attitude that she'd felt insulted instead of complimented.

"Nicholas, maybe *you're* the one who's had too much booze, to think you can say what you just said and not get a lollipop stuck to your Dolce & Gabbana suit."

"Add funny," he said, his tone reminiscent of the way he'd distractedly fielded her conversation in the casino. "You're hot and funny."

Brushed off, dismissed, Ona stared blindly at her lollipop. Get rid of the candy, get the man.

She made sure he watched her as she held up the lollipop and stuck it into her mouth.

Nicholas responded to her defiance with a slight narrowing of his beautiful eyes and a casual one-shouldered shrug.

A frantic "Excuse me!" had heads twisting and voices pausing. Regan was crossing and uncrossing her arms nervously. "I—I think I messed up. There's a bed in here, not a massage table. Everyone from PAAC, we should go."

"Regan, I turned off my phone, got a bracelet and took a seat," someone said. "You can leave, but I'm staying here."

Others echoed the sentiment, and admirably taking a stand, Regan Waltz got up, directed a cold stare in Ona's direction, reclaimed her phone and walked out. The doors closed, echoing.

Moments later from a side entrance emerged a slim woman wearing a white shirt and leather pants with her dark hair in a ponytail. Introducing herself as Sephora, she drifted from a brief chat about essential oils to a short list of rules and gently reminded that security was present to assist anyone who exhibited difficulty adhering to those rules.

"Our bed is memory foam over a gel mattress, designed to enhance participants' comfort," she said, peeling back a corner of the bedding. "The sheets are freshly washed and have been scented with rosemary and peppermint essential oils."

Sephora scanned the room and the amber lights touched the gems on her double left eyebrow piercings. "Would a male and a female volunteer join me, please? For yoni massage demonstration purposes, I'll guide the male in focusing on the female and giving the proper respect to her core."

"Yoni massage?" Ona whispered. Noting the sea of puzzled faces, and plenty that appeared unfazed, she found Nicholas inconspicuously text messaging on his smartphone. "Security took your phone," she murmured. "How'd you get it back?"

"Security took my work phone. This's my personal phone."

How uncharacteristically devious of him.

"Can the personal texts wait until after the workshop? We're about to be schooled in tantric sex."

"What sex?"

"Tantric. Before security confiscates your phone, open Google and search *yoni massage*."

Complying, Nicholas processed the search and knit his brows. "As cool as that sounds, I'm gonna need you to give me a play-by-play later, Ona. I need to go."

"Go? But what happened to being in this together? Nick?" Finally Ona stopped talking, because he didn't stop once to hear her out as he pocketed his phone and made a fast departure.

Gazing at his empty chair, then straight ahead at the bed dominating the room, she felt clarity pierce her decade-old crush and seduction schemes. This was the first time Nicholas Callaghan had ever looked at Ona,

and he hadn't liked what he'd seen: a "hot" woman ru-
ining herself with calories.

*Do you want to be unseen tonight? An invisible
woman sitting next to an empty chair?*

Ona's clothes were suddenly suffocating her, and
she didn't know what she'd do if she couldn't escape
this seat. Freeing herself, she shot her hand in the air
and sought the only freedom she'd find in this room.

A silk-covered bed.

Ona was already perched at the end of it, fixating on
the contrast of the sheets' deep colors against her Burberry skirt, when she heard a man say, "I'll volunteer."

Riker!

Deaf to everyone but the stranger who'd become
more of a friend to her than the people she'd stepped
onto *The Lure* with, she was ecstatic as tears flocked
to her eyes.

"I'm her man," he said, "and I volunteer."

"Are you comfortable sharing this with him?" Sephora
asked Ona as they watched him emerge from a rear row
in jeans, a T-shirt and a determined stare that Ona felt
clear to her bone marrow.

"I am."

Sephora took Ona's hand and laid it in Riker's. "Gently undress her, but don't rush. Never rush her. This is
less of a sex act, and more of a moment of bonding."

Kneeling, Riker began to strip her. He started with
her shoes, then leaned close as he began to unbutton
her shirt. "I saw him leave you here," he whispered.

"He doesn't see me," she mumbled around the champagne lollipop. "None of them do." Embarrassing, but
true.

"They will."

Ona looked past him. Peppered throughout the mass

of strangers were her former classmates. They'd spent four years together, yet none of them had ever seen—really seen—her.

You'll see me now.

Riker soothed her jitters with his sexy smirk as he revealed her bra...

You're going to see the lumpectomy scar I talked about with nobody but the guy touching me now.

He stroked her arms as Sephora brought a tray of oil to the bed and, positioning herself behind Ona and taking the champagne lollipop to taste for herself, unhooked the bra...

Riker let Ona's shirt and bra join her shoes, guided her to lift her hips so he could tug off the skirt and undies...

You're going to see this man give me more respect than anyone's ever given me.

Ona didn't close her eyes. She watched the others watch her, until carnality demanded her complete attention.

"Trust," Sephora murmured, kissing her shoulder. She'd freed her hair and it swept over Ona's skin and tangled with her own. "Trust him to show you what you deserve. Breathe deeply and feel him."

Riker's hands, glistening in oil, glided over her body, and Ona was faintly aware of Sephora abandoning her on the bed.

"Apply deeper pressure on the pea-size knots of tension throughout her form," the woman instructed softly, going to his side. She kissed his neck. "Deeper. Deeper... Good."

Ona's muscles began to relax and her mind centered on him. There was no music. There was no audience. There was no Sephora. There was only Riker, discovering her and owning her and making her wonder what it might feel like to let him love her.

Settling between her legs, he massaged her and she opened her eyes to meet his.

Ona inhaled as Riker's touch became more intimate. Lightly he pinched her flesh. And then, with his blue eyes darker than she'd ever seen them, he slid two fingers firmly inside.

It was a struggle to caress the sheets instead of push his hand away. She'd never had this type of soul-deep pleasure, knew without asking that he'd never given it. This was new to them both.

Gradually, he began to stroke faster. The glide of his slick fingers, the slap of friction, became all she could hear.

Trust him...

Trusting him, and trusting what they were sharing, Ona let herself relax into an orgasm. It hit with seismic intensity, grabbing her entire body, and she found herself soaked with emotions, oil and wet arousal.

Shaking, she said his name. "Riker. Just..."

Somehow he understood her, and wasn't that the point—to reach a previously untasted flavor of understanding? Grabbing her clothes, he came back to the bed and carried her stark-naked out of the VIP room.

Chapter 5

When *The Lure* arrived at port the next morning, Ona was among the last to leave the ship. It wasn't because Riker Ewan had kept her busy. On the contrary, after last night's tantric sex workshop, he'd brought her to her cabin, pressed her hand to his rigid erection and said in the most tortured tones she'd ever heard, "What are we gonna do, Ona?" and when neither of them had a damn answer, he'd kissed her and left. This morning she'd woken up to a slow sunrise, a ringing phone and a dinging tablet, because no one in her group could seem to process that she wasn't responsible for planning everyone's individual excursions and couldn't play go-between the entire day. A full day on the Bahamas awaited the passengers, and the only scheduled activities for the PAAC brats were a photo session in front of Balcony House for PAAC's newsletter and a laid-back dinner on Paradise Island. Aside from that, she'd need to make sure her group returned to *The Lure* before departure.

Wearing a pink lace bikini beneath denim cutoffs and an off-the-shoulder white gauzy shirt, Ona fluffed her already poofy high ponytail and tapped her eye-glasses frames as she joined her group for the gorgeous complimentary buffet breakfast Guest Services had arranged at the cafeteria-style pier restaurant. She intended to get in the Bahamian water today, swim a lit-tle, splash around a lot, and didn't want the hassle of worrying about keeping her hair straight and sand out of her contacts.

"Ona, c'mon over here," Jane called from one of the three rustic tables their group occupied. Seated be-side her, Regan appeared reluctant to move her hand-bag from the chair Jane indicated. "We have mimosas."

Carrying her tray to their table, she saw the others exchange knowing glances. "What is it?"

"You look *amazing*," Jane gushed.

"The glasses?" Ona bit into her powdered sugar toast.

"No."

"The natural hair?" She tugged a springy lock.

Jane picked up her mimosa, considering Ona. "No again. Few things can put sparkle like that in a woman's eyes. One of them is a thorough orgasm. Lucky you."

Regan ignored her untouched mimosa for a lipstick-stained carton of milk and said, "Exhibitionism, Ona? Just seems a little over-the-top."

"The yoni massage wasn't exhibitionism," Jane cor-rected. "It doesn't mean those of us who stayed behind have a voyeurism fetish. If we did, so what?" She began to dissect her corned beef hash. "That massage was the most sensual thing I've ever watched. It was art, and it was so beautiful. I cried. Ask Cole. He was sitting next to me, and he was very much…inspired by it."

Conversation continued, and Ona slumped on the bench, her gaze sweeping the table to her left and the one to her right. Cole Stanwyck was seated beside Rajon Sneed, and when she caught a few legal phrases she was relieved that they weren't discussing her. She'd succeeded in becoming visible to a handful of people she hadn't socialized with in years. After their entire class's high school reunion in August, another decade would probably pass before she saw any of them again. Life moved along that way, and her main regret in this moment was that she hadn't realized it sooner.

Last night, Riker Ewan had mattered. He still did, and the memories of his hands manipulating her body began to drench her with a heated dampness and a greed for more. She didn't want him for pretend. She didn't want the lie they'd built together. She didn't want to make Nicholas Callaghan jealous.

She had the answer now—she knew that whatever had brought Riker to her that first day on *The Lure* and whatever her heart demanded were in total agreement.

Ona searched the restaurant but didn't see him. Tonight's departure seemed an eternity away, but she couldn't very well text *I'm having a great time sightseeing. By the way, I think we should be together for real.*

Eating only a portion of her breakfast, she, for the umpteenth time, saw Regan ogle the bacon on her plate. Casually, she wrapped a strip in a napkin, knelt beside Regan's chair and whispered, "Regan, you're a WASP. If your love/hate relationship with bacon isn't a religious issue, am I right in guessing it's a dietary issue?"

"I don't know what you're talking about."

"Did you adore Porky Pig growing up and now feel guilty about wanting bacon?"

"Ona, you're obnoxious."

"That may be. But am I right?"

Regan put down her milk carton. "It's complicated."

"That's quite the generic response, but I won't push you. Open your hand under the table. *Regan*, just do it." When the woman uncurled her fingers, Ona set the napkin on her palm. "It's a strip of bacon. Eat it or not. Just thought I'd offer it."

Regan looked at her, her eyes conflicted. Then she balled up the napkin and dumped it onto her breakfast tray. "I don't want a Fishtown girl's charity. Go away now."

Hate wasn't the answer to hate, and there was something combustible brewing beneath Regan Waltz's surface. So instead of dumping the woman's mimosa on her head, Ona said calmly, "There's nothing shameful about charity. I wouldn't have attended PAAC if not for that scholarship, and where would any of us be without someone—whether a stranger or our own parents—to help us out once in a while?"

"Don't talk circles around me," Regan snapped, and folks' attention gravitated to them.

"Maybe you should quit standing in the same place. Then it wouldn't be so easy to do."

"What does *that* mean?"

"It just means I'm done with this, Regan. I'm going forward. High school was ten years ago, and the best part of that experience for me died in Alaska. Unless I screwed up by going after the wrong things, I have a shot at something good in my life. I really need that, so hopefully you can understand that I won't waste another minute bitching this out with you. See you at Balcony House for the picture."

Ona went to the restroom to wash her hands…and to make sure her heart hadn't dropped out of her ass.

What had just happened? She'd gone head-to-head against Regan Waltz in the most civilized manner she could dream up. No yelling, no petty insults, no hurtful swipes, no hate.

After leaving a tip in the mason jar for the attendant, Ona left the restroom with the sole purpose of getting a private moment with Riker before she was due at Balcony House. Already the whole lot of them were cutting it close, lingering over the buffet.

Spotting Cole waiting for her outside the restroom, she determined she wouldn't let him delay her in getting to Riker.

"What can I do for you, Cole?"

"Hey, is that a bona fide offer, Stilts?"

"Is there something—regarding the reunion—that I can help you with?"

"This is the situation, Ona. Last night you walked into that VIP room with Nicholas's arm around you, but you left with some other man. I want some of what he got. What do I need to do?"

Nudging past him, she said, "Insulting me isn't the way to get my attention. Nicholas and I have never hooked up, and I decided that we never will. There's one man for me. Only one. It's not Nick. It's not you, Cole. And…it wasn't even Matty."

"Do you have any idea how much money I play with? How much does the other guy make?"

"Doesn't matter." Cole designed apps and Riker tended bar. It couldn't make Cole a superior man. Riker and Ona had a connection that had begun before they'd truly laid eyes on each other, and with every word, look and unspoken thought between them, that connection had deepened. "I'm in love with *him*, not his paycheck."

"Love?" Cole laughed. "I'll do you a favor and for-

get you said that. If you loved him, you wouldn't have been sitting on Nicholas's lap the other night."

Ona hadn't loved Riker that night. She did now, but she wouldn't waste much more time convincing Cole when he wasn't the man who mattered. "I don't want *you*, though. Never have. Sometimes we think we can make it work with the wrong people, and all it does is cause unnecessary hurt. I'm not going to hurt you, Cole, and don't you try to hurt me by keeping at this."

Cole didn't stop her, but by the time she made it to the cafeteria everyone from PAAC had geared up to leave and she and Cole made for an awkward pair, straggling behind and earning some suggestive looks and uncalled-for remarks.

The lot of them didn't break up until after they met with a photographer at Balcony House. Posing in front of the centuries-old pink Market Street house, they all smiled brilliantly for the camera. For some the cheer was genuine. For others, namely Ona, whom at six-one was made to stand between Nicholas and Cole, it was feigned.

After the photos, some sought the cannons of Fort Fincastle while others escaped to Blue Lagoon Island. Ona went directly to Atlantis. Guided tours and souvenir shopping were wonderful things, but she valued the separation and didn't mind trading some excursion opportunities for breathing room.

She visited the resort concierge first to make sure there were no wrinkles in her arrangements for an al-fresco dinner. All was confirmed, and finding herself with no coordinator duties for the next few hours, she let herself be a tourist. In the resort casino she gambled away the equivalent of fifty US dollars, then won it back to break even. Afterward she stood outside in

the breathless beauty and dreamlike luxury and came
to understand that she was unfulfilled. What she'd told
Cole in the pier restaurant had been immensely true.
She needed more than money to know happiness. It
didn't matter that Cole and Nicholas wouldn't blink an
eye at places like Atlantis while Riker valued a buck.

It only mattered that Riker was her necessity and
luxury, and she needed to be in his arms.

I need to see you, she texted. What you asked me
last night. I have my answer.

A short reply came only a shard of a moment later.
Ona knew, because she'd been fiddling with her glasses,
waiting with her heart beating in her throat.

Where are you?

Atlantis. Meet me at the rope bridge.

Going to the bridge, Ona saw a smattering of tour-
ists snapping photos. She panned her camera along the
stretch of the bridge, lingering on the pattern of the
rope, the rushing waterfall and the spectacular gleam
of sunlight on the water. She'd send the video to her
parents and make them swear to visit Nassau once they
exhausted all the US sites on their must-visit list.

"Hey."

Ona lowered her phone, swallowing hard and turning
toward that sexy Boston voice. It was a reincarnation
of their first meeting, only he stood feet away and she
could appreciate him all at once. She needed to twirl
her fingers in his dark blond hair, wrap her legs around
his hips, kiss him uninhibitedly—because a kiss last
night hadn't been enough.

And his hands. She needed to worship the hands that had worshipped her.

There was no time for hesitation or backpedaling. Only time for taking a chance on this man, taking a risk on happiness and taking everything he could give her.

"I know the answer," she said, sprinting across the quivering bridge until she could leap and land exactly where she belonged. In his arms, she took off his sunglasses, grappled gracelessly at his shirt, circled her legs around his waist and breathed in his scent of simmering sunshine against spicy, citrusy cologne. "I'm gonna run with this. That's what I want to do. I want to take whatever's between us and run with it."

"Ona." Riker's strong hands clutched her ass. His mouth trapped hers, and they kissed as though battling for dominance or survival. Biting lightly. Licking fiercely. Demanding more. "We don't know each other."

"We *understand* each other," she said, gasping in air, dizzy with lust and love and joy and fear. "You said you prefer it. Guess what, Riker? So do I."

"If I said to you, 'Ona, when we get off the ship in Miami I want you to come with me,' would you do it? Would you pass up Philadelphia and New York and come to Boston with a guy who serves drinks and sweeps up a floor?"

"Yes," she said roughly. Certain. Convinced. Probably crazy.

"Yes?"

"Yes, if that guy is you. I'm not asking for forever. I'm not jumping ahead like that. But I didn't want to find myself watching you walk away on that pier in Miami, not knowing that for me this is more than pretend or some half-baked plan to find myself with someone else."

Again with the quiet stare. This time she held it and didn't falter. "Ona, don't let some stranger you met on a cruise twist your life. I'm saying it again, and I want you to listen. We don't know each other. Damn it, you don't know me."

"What don't I know, then?" she challenged. "What fact about you is going to change how I feel? You made me feel this way. I can't stop it. I don't want to."

"You don't know my scars," he grunted. "You haven't seen my scars."

Ona unfolded her legs, then her feet touched the bridge. She handed him back his sunglasses. "Then let's change that."

The sugary white sand was hot beneath her bare feet as she walked beside Riker on the beach. She waited until they moved beneath the sheltering shadows of a grouping of palm trees before she dropped her sandals and said, "I'm done waiting for things to happen. I can't wait for this. So show me, right here."

Riker studied her through his dark lenses, then he yanked his shirt over his head and tossed it onto the sand at her feet. He was all flexing muscles and taut limbs, all intense, tightly controlled male, and she wanted everything.

Ona lifted a heavy muscled arm, coasted her fingers over his marred flesh. It was a palette of whites and reds and violets. The scars, smooth in some spots but raised in others, began at his armpit and appeared to overlap straight down to his hip bone. They made her think of pain, of screams void of sound and of nightmares. At the same time, they made her think of miracles and sacrifice and courage.

Bending, she traced a raised scar with her lips.

Added a light lick. "You're incredible," she said, repeating what he'd said to her in Sirens' Song.

He gripped her hair. "I really need to get my hands tangled in this."

Ona pulled the silk tie free, whipped her curls left then right and let it tumble. She sighed when his hands plowed through her hair to guide her head to his. He met her with a kiss that shattered her boundaries. His teeth caught her lips, his tongue writhed against hers. She was hardly aware of his hand sliding around to her neck, then settling on her shirt collar.

Riker's mouth left hers, and she felt robbed of something precious. "How fast can you take this off?"

She stripped off her shirt and, taking it further, discarded her cutoffs. Down to her lace bikini, she asked, "Fast enough?"

Dropping to his knees in the sand, in this semi-secluded paradise, he took off his sunglasses and kissed her abdomen. His lips sucked at her skin, his stubble grazed her, his teeth teased. As his mouth moved over her, his hands went inside her bikini bottoms to squeeze her butt. The sensual play of his mouth was echoed with the dirty maneuvering of his hands. "I have condoms, Ona."

"Then—" she reached behind her to spring loose the bikini top's ties "—I have one demand. Don't stop."

Bringing her down to the sand, he unfastened his jeans. He wanted her to handle him, and that was what she would do. No holding back and no remorse. She pushed his shoulders until he was lying on his back, and after she had him naked between the sun and sand, she gently dragged her fingernails down his torso and watched his shaft leap reflexively. Massaging his pelvis and thighs, she charmed his stiff flesh…

"You've been getting me hard like this every day, Ona. Every day I see you, I end up like this."

"Today's different." And then she kissed him intimately. Bowing between his legs, she maintained a steady, relentless pace, coming up for one last declaration. "Today we don't stop."

Easing up, licking her lips, she watched and listened as he groaned, cussed and pounded his fists into the sand. She felt her temperature rise and her skin dampen. Sand started to stick to her, but she didn't care as he spun her around and pinned her.

Indolently, he pinched her breasts and tongued each nipple. The more she squirmed against the sensation, the more deliberately he teased her. "I knew that first day you would taste good. Now tell me," he said, removing her bottoms, "Ona, are you wet for me?"

"I am. I swear it." Spreading her thighs, bringing them up so she could grip her calves, she would let him discover for himself. "It's for you. I thought it could be for someone else, but it can't."

"Tell me again this is for me." His mouth moved down her body. "Tell me you're for me."

"It is. I am. I swear, Riker."

Opening her with his fingers and shoving her to chaos with his tongue, he dined until he had her sweating from the heat and her own arousal. She watched her hips roll, watched herself come against his open mouth. And she impatiently waited for him to share her taste. He trailed kisses up her rib cage, to her nipples that were dark from his hands and teeth. Her mouth was parted and ready for his when he reached her, and he slipped his tongue inside.

Riker let her lick into his mouth, and she was aware

of the condom package tearing open. "Sure you still want this to happen? Want me to do you?"

Ona's lips parted but no sound came out. So she steadied his erection and ground against him, meeting him, needing him exactly like this. And yeah, he did know her. He knew how to lean against her and thrust to inflict almost painful pleasure. He knew to cradle her and to move his mouth silkily over hers as he rocked her deeper into the sand.

Afterward, Ona made it back into her lace bottoms only, and Riker into his jeans, and they were sandy and sticky and too hot to stay in one place. Together, his arm slung over her shoulders and hers wrapped around his waist, they started walking deeper into the protection of the trees.

"Ona."

Nicholas, in his polo shirt and khakis, so clean and expensive, stood in their path. His gaze stalled on her breasts long enough for Riker to find it appropriate to dip and lick one of her nipples and murmur, "Ona, want to tell your old friend here that you're busy?"

"She's busy doing what?" Nicholas said venomously.

"Private school education and you can't figure that out for yourself?"

"Son of a—"

"Nick, please leave," Ona interrupted. "Riker and I are busy, so if you don't mind… Actually, I don't care whether you mind or not. I'm on my own time right now, but I'll see you and everyone else at dinner." Changing course, she began to lead Riker in the other direction.

But he stopped her. "You said that to piss him off or to make him jealous?"

"I'm done with that plan," she insisted. "I don't want to make him jealous anymore."

"You say that, but he shows up and… Look, about this." Riker cupped her between the legs, and tense, fascinated, she absorbed every sensation. "Ona, I'm not gonna share it. I'm not sharing you with anybody. Are you okay with that?'

"Yeah. Nicholas is the past."

"All of a sudden? I thought we were being real with each other."

"I am. It's all of a sudden, but that's the truth. There are no lies."

Riker didn't seem convinced. But after a solemn, "All right," he picked her up and put her over one shoulder and then started to jog toward the water. "If we're in the business of not lying, then let's make what you told Saint Nick true."

Ona didn't say no when Riker booked them a suite at the Cove Atlantis. They'd walked in damp, disheveled and speckled with grains of sand, and because Nicholas had already found her topless and wrapped around Riker, she didn't want to show up to dinner carrying bold evidence of how she'd spent her day at port. While their clothes were being cleaned, she and Riker took turns showering and fell asleep tangled up in sheets with the TV turned to a 1970s American sitcom and the windows open to the ocean.

Room service woke them up, and they shared a pair of beers before they finally dressed and joined the PAAC brats.

"So glad you could make it to dinner," someone said sarcastically as she and Riker claimed a pair of seats at one of the elegantly dressed outdoor tables.

"I'll pass on the snark, thanks," she said brightly. "I'd rather have an appetizer."

"Ignore the haters," Jane advised. "The sex fairies are kind to you. Be glad."

Ona tried to eat her four-course meal and not care about anything except the fact that she had a new man in her life, but it was difficult when every time she looked up, she found Nicholas observing her while muttering to someone else. What right did he think he had to believe she owed him anything outside of her direct duties as reunion coordinator? Time and again she'd tried to work for his attention, but he'd refused her every attempt. He didn't want her, and she deserved better than what he could give. Finally she got Riker's simple point: she deserved better.

She was worthy of more than the males from her high school society, from her childhood, could offer her. It didn't make them wrong or her problematic. It only meant that they weren't meant to be.

Stepping into a hallway on an erotic ship and meeting a man who'd open her mind and body to new experiences and ideas? *That* was meant to be. It was too unexplainable to be anything else.

After dinner and a rowdy round of drinks, somebody got the reckless idea to give one of the empty wine bottles a spin on the patio. Recruiting resort staff to help clear the center of the space, the men encouraged the women to risk getting their outfits dirty for the sake of a game you just didn't turn down.

"Is this Spin the Bottle or Seven Minutes in Heaven?" Ona wanted to clarify as she sat down next to Rajon's wheelchair. "Since we're apparently spinning the bottle and sneaking off to the pool for seven minutes with the poor bastard the bottle lands on?"

"It's an amalgamation," Rajon said. "No one's obligated to get their freak on. Go to the pool and talk, play

Rock, Paper, Scissors—doesn't matter. If you want a quickie, more power to you. Seven minutes is all you get."

Cole spun first, and the bottle pointed at someone else's wife. They disappeared for seven minutes and when they returned to the circle, her husband erupted from a bitter combination of too many drinks and too many questions. Bickering, they left the circle and went into the resort.

"Tighten the circle," Regan said. "It's my turn." When she spun, the bottle stopped with the nose pointed squarely at Ona.

"Oh, can we watch?" a man pleaded.

"No," Regan replied at the same time that Ona said, "I'm not going to the pool with her."

"I want to do it," Regan insisted. "But we need privacy. So no one's watching anything."

Ona looked to Riker, shrugging as she got to her feet and trailed Regan to the pool. "So how would you like to spend the next seven minutes?"

The woman was silent for a few moments. Then her shoulders heaved.

Uh-oh. "Regan? Wh-what's wrong? It's just seven measly minutes. Nothing to bawl over."

"What you're doing with Nicholas… Is this retaliation for something I did to you in high school? Was I cruel to you?"

"You dominated, Regan. A lot of times dominating means skimping on the friendliness. But that's high school, and I told you earlier at the pier that I'm over that."

"Why, Ona? Because you have what you want? You have Nicholas?"

"I don't *have* anyone. If you want to know whether

or not he's—oh, how'd you put it the other day?—*boffing* me, the answer's no. I'm with someone else, and I care about this person."

"Nicholas has been telling people that you showed him your breasts on the beach."

"I was topless on the beach because I was sharing something intimate with Riker. Nicholas found us, that's all. Tell him to get over it. If you and he would've stayed in that workshop yesterday, you both would've gotten a look-see right along with everyone else."

"Don't you care about that, being looked at?"

She used to. She'd declined auditioning for *Hair* because of the nudity. Now… "Not particularly. Not anymore."

"Could you tone it down around Nicholas Callaghan?"

"Why, Regan?" Suspicious, Ona searched the woman's eyes. "What the hell is happening with you? He's a single man—"

"Wrong!" Tears started to trickle. "*Wrong.* He's not single. Nicholas is with me. We're engaged, Ona. Have been for over a year."

Ona sank to a chaise longue. "You must be screwing with me this time."

"I'm not. He hasn't told his family yet. They lost a ton in an awful business venture and have been wanting him to marry strategically. That makes me unsuitable. He says he'll tell them, but timing is everything." Regan sat next to her. "Time is something he and I don't have anymore. I'm pregnant."

"My lord. Did you sit on the upper deck or something?"

Pushing back her golden curls, Regan laughed. "Uh-uh, that's not it. I didn't know I was pregnant until yesterday. I bought a test at the ship's pharmacy."

"Well, it's not confirmed, then."

"It could be a false positive, but I don't think so. I think I'm pregnant by a man who's too afraid to tell his family that he's going to marry me." Her mouth curled and she gripped Ona's hands. "Part of me doesn't want him, Ona. He's been flirting with you from the minute he saw you in Miami, and it's been killing me. And he's selfish—so selfish. Most of the time when we're together, he treats me like a blow-up doll. *That's* why I have tension in my neck, because all he wants is—"

"I—I get it." Ona was going to be sick in this pool. Damn, had she been off the mark. Saint Nick was a bastard. It didn't seem plausible, but then again, he'd shown Ona similar tendencies. Their moments together had been starkly one-sided.

"He won't let me eat bacon."

Okay, now that was just wicked. "What do you mean, he won't let you?"

"He says he doesn't want me to be fat. It's for my own welfare."

Oh, God. It *was* true. "Regan—"

"Seven minutes," a man hollered out to the pool. He swaggered over to them. "Y'all make out?"

"No," Ona said while Regan turned away to wipe her tears.

"Would you?"

"Oh, get over it," Regan huffed, then she grabbed Ona's face, kissed her cheek and whispered, "Hey, this stays between you and me. Don't tell anybody about Nick or the engagement or the baby." Brushing past him, she paused to kiss him full on the lips. "There. Report that to everyone. I'm going inside for bacon."

Ona rocked slowly, then got up and sought Riker.

"Can we go back to *The Lure*? I just want to be with somebody I can trust. I need you right now."

"C'mon."

Walking beside him, she looked back at the gathering to find Nicholas watching her with the empty wine bottle in his hand.

Chapter 6

"What are you drinking? A Miller? Let me buy you another."

Riker, wound tight since he'd lied straight to Ona's face yesterday in the Bahamas, didn't budge on his stool in the ever-packed Sirens' Song. He didn't have to. He knew the man who'd approached him at the bar was part of Ona's group—Cole Stanwyck, the son of a bitch who'd been getting in her way.

"I got my beer under control," he said calmly.

"Guy, listen, all you need to do is overtip the waitress for the first drink. She'll be hooking you up in no time. Trust me, I know how the more upscale places run. Hell, with my money, I could own this ship."

Riker gave his head a quarter turn. "Is that right?"

"That's right. Get inside a certain tax bracket and you learn these things. You learn things about women, too. What they're really after." Cole put his elbow on the bar, making himself comfortable. "Take Stilts Tracy. She's had her eye on our classmate Nicholas since high school. You may be dipping your wick in her now, but it's always been Nicholas for her. I'd tell you to ask her friend Matty Grillo all about it, but seeing as most of him's in a jar on somebody's mantel, that makes things a little complicated logistically."

"Ona and I are all right."

"You think that, but what you don't know about Ona is she's from Fishtown. We all had some good times with her way back when, but she's not trying to go back to Fishtown or anyplace like it. She's all about moving up in the world. Designer labels, pricey liquor, things men like me can give her without breaking the bank."

"Thanks for the tip. But I give her the kind of pleasure that make her forget about designer labels and pricey liquor, and that seems to work out pretty good for us." Riker's phone rang and vibrated, and when he pulled it from his pocket, he had to snatch it from Cole's view. "Take the stool. Buy yourself a nice pricey drink there."

Riker took the call outside the lounge. "Thought I'd hear from you before now, Kate."

Kate Russ greeted him with an expletive. "Damn you, Riker. For someone so underhanded, you certainly were sloppy about it, using your trust fund to get yourself a cabin on the ship *and* a suite at the Atlantis. The accountant managing the fund noticed the uncharacteristic activity and contacted me."

"He could've saved you the trouble and just contacted me."

"It's my money."

"Yeah, Kate? All these years it's been collecting and

you've been pushing me to spend it, swearing that it's the proof of what a generous, loving mother you are."

Kate sighed laboriously. "It *is* your money, but I'm the one who put it there for you. I know why you're on *The Lure*, and it's to hurt me."

"You and I were scheduled to meet up at headquarters. You pissed on that, so I needed to come up with a new plan. This ship's not being managed well."

"That's your assessment, but—"

"A group of private school folks are on this ship instead of *The Lore*. Can't blame it on the *o* and the *u*. Management, Guest Services, they screwed up and pinned it all on one of the guests."

"Excuse me?" Kate squeaked. "Private schoolers."

"Whoa, hold up, Kate. *Former* private schoolers. It was supposed to be a reunion trip. The ship's been doling out big-money conveniences to butter them up, especially the one who's holding the bag. All of this is happening and you have no clue."

"This ship is my baby, Riker."

"And you abandoned it, not the least bit aware of how it's getting by. Wouldn't be the first time you did that."

"I did not abandon you. Emory raised you properly and he kept me informed. You want to punish me for... Okay, I realize I've made so many mistakes with you, but it's easy to make a mistake when you just can't see the right way to go." Kate paused. "I'm sorry. I don't know if I ever said that, but I've always thought it. I'm sorry, Riker, and I want us to talk."

It was Riker's turn to pause. "I don't know."

"Please...don't take my mistakes out on *The Lure*. That ship has brought together people who've fallen in love and stayed in love. Those people have the kind of happiness that I didn't have—the kind you didn't even have with Marisol."

Riker rubbed his eyes. He was weary. "Kate, I don't know what I'm going to do about this ship." But he knew with the entirety of his heart that she was right about *The Lure*'s track record in hooking people up.

Fallen in love... Yeah, he was definitely there. He'd been in love before. He'd loved Marisol, but now he loved Ona, and he loved her in a way that made him want to give more of himself.

Stayed in love... About that. His chances of keeping up what he'd found with Ona were slim if he couldn't show her what he'd failed to show Marisol.

Honesty.

Ona reported to *The Lure*'s top-tier ballroom early. Armed with her tablet and smartphone and outfitted in stilettos and a gown with a gemstone bodice and fluttery aquamarine skirt—a splurge she'd needed to increase her credit card's limit to accommodate—she graciously allowed a crew to open the gigantic doors.

Perfection welcomed her. To think that she'd been a bundle of nerves while getting dressed earlier. Guest Services had contacted her hours ago to report an upgrade in the venue for her party's private ball. The four-piece orchestra and decorations had been relocated and the food would be catered to the new location.

Ona had personally contacted each stateroom and spa suite of those in her group, doing her best to explain the change when even she didn't know why the ship had extended such a courtesy. Then she'd finished her hair and makeup and texted Riker that for him she was saving a slow dance…and any dance that might make grinding appropriate.

The ballroom, simply called Romance, was a place of silvery wall coverings and finely polished teak and accents of crystal and diamonds. Lights were strung across the high ceiling and wrapped around columns and artificial plants. The fragrance teasing the air was something Ona couldn't describe, but it made her think of magic. She had only a minute to stand still and let the perfection of it all hit her before she was drawn into last-minute details.

A live orchestra, dancing and a catered dinner to close this cruise with a classy, memorable treat. It was crafted in a style that PAAC would approve of, tame and elegant. But Ona had been the after-party girl once— and she still was, because she could hardly wait to have a private after-party with Riker Ewan. They'd spend tonight in his cabin, where her classmates couldn't so easily disturb her, and in the morning she would step onto the Miami pier with him.

"Spectacular," a woman proclaimed, and Ona stepped away from the orchestra assembled in a white-gold corner of the ballroom.

"Quinn," Ona said, greeting the guest services manager with a handshake. "Thanks—but I didn't do all of this."

"You did. I saw the design images you emailed with your request to reserve the other ballroom. It was a stunning vision. I'm glad our staff was able to help you realize it."

"Thank you for this ballroom. This on top of the other favors, it's almost too much, really."

"*The Lure* can't take credit for the upgrade. Didn't Guest Services clarify? Someone at Stewart-Russ sent down the request." Concern touched Quinn's eyes. "Ms. Tracy, have you had an enjoyable cruise?"

"Yes," Ona confessed. "I met someone. I wouldn't have met him on *The Lore*."

"Ah. I'd wondered if you'd submitted a complaint to Stewart-Russ. The way you've handled this situation is admirable, to say the least."

"Yeah? *Admirable* isn't how my academy's going to put it when it blacklists me in the event planning industry."

"That would be tragic. Stewart-Russ is often deficient in dynamic, creative, adaptable staff." Quinn hesitated. "Enjoy the night, Ms. Tracy. Thank you for choosing *The Lure*."

I'm starting to think The Lure *chose me*, Ona quietly returned, watching Quinn adjust a waiter's tie and motion to someone else to fix a crooked plant leaf as she left the ballroom.

Going to the table where she'd set her tablet and phone, Ona halted as a tuxedoed Nicholas cut her off. Reaching the table first, he picked up the devices and held them out without actually relinquishing them.

"When did you become so beautiful, Ona?"

Ona scoffed. "I don't think you were looking that day." She reached for the tablet and phone, but he captured her hand and pressed it to his mouth, kissing and abrading her with his teeth while his green eyes held her. "Stop, Nicholas. I don't want you to touch me like that. Regan wouldn't want you to, either."

"What does Regan have to do with this?"

"A man should at least consider his fiancée before he goes about trying to screw another woman." Ona pulled her hand away then wrestled her things from him. "You're hurting her. You're driving her away."

"Regan's my responsibility."

Yeah, and if she's pregnant then that baby's your re-

sponsibility, too. "Act like it, then. Commit to her and stop controlling her."

Nicholas frowned, made another grab for her, and she slapped his wrist away. "Ona… Now you're out of line. It's not your fault," he continued, because apparently he lacked the sense to shut up. "Your upbringing's not your fault. It's, what, a Fishtown thing? A black community thing?"

Upbringing. A Fishtown thing. A black community thing.

Ona gasped, and unable to stop the tears flocking to her eyes, she twisted around to see if anyone had overheard him.

No one met her glance, but she needed no one's backup.

Jet out of there? She wouldn't do it.

Cuss him out? She wouldn't do that, either.

But she recoiled as the words sank into her flesh. She wanted to scrub her skin where he'd touched her. She hadn't kissed him, but she wanted to rinse her mouth, anyway.

And her dreams. Those silly, stupid teenage dreams of sex and laughter? She wanted to erase them.

As he stalked out of the ballroom she felt more sad than angry. Sad for him, because how unfortunate to be utterly, incorrigibly ignorant. Sad for herself, because she'd once chosen "saint" Nicholas over Matty Grillo and Riker Ewan.

A server rushed to her before the ballroom doors shut in Nicholas's wake. "I can call for security, ma'am."

"No, it's done," Ona assured him. "It was just a disagreement with an old friend."

"Me? If I wanted friends like that, I'd get myself some enemies," he commented, casting a glance at the doors before he resumed arranging centerpieces on the linen-draped tables.

Laying the incident aside, Ona submerged herself in work. Over the next hour her classmates, their significant others and the shipboard staff entered the ballroom to lively interpretations of the most popular songs in their PAAC glee club cohort's repertoire. A bartending crew wheeled an impressive champagne trolley, and only when it arrived at Ona's table did she finally take her seat and accept the shower of compliments and appreciative remarks.

"I need to see you alone," Riker said, straddling the chair beside hers. "When can we do that?"

Ona wanted it to be now. He was too hot not to touch in that casual suit with the open collar. She dipped her fingers into the opening, toying at his dog tags, taking an excuse to fondle him. "After drinks we can disappear. If we skip foreplay, we can be back before dinner."

"Damn. Ona—"

"Everybody have a drink?" Turning, Ona found Cole Stanwyck behind a microphone with a champagne glass held high. "I know we're supposed to be coming up here and talking about our best glee club memories, but I think we should start by giving our reunion coordinator some props. Stilts—sorry, *Ona*—stand up for me."

She stood and gave the room a smile, but when she started to sit again, Cole interrupted.

"Up, Ona. Keep standing. We're all going to applaud you. The majority of the club had an all right time, so we'd call that a success, wouldn't we? Congratulations on pulling off your first event planning job." At the surge of confused comments and questions, he said, "Oh, did you think she was a legitimate event planner? Well, she's not. She lied to us and to PAAC."

Ona bit the inside of her cheek. Shaking her head at Cole, she had no words.

"Ona Tracy was terminated from an advertising firm in New York and hasn't pulled a paycheck since. She misrepresented herself to our school, got the account and experimented with our reunion cruise." Feigning sincerity, Cole cocked his head at Ona. "But we can't blame her for botching our reservations. Apparently that wasn't her fault after all. That's the company's bad."

"How do you know that?" she demanded, managing the words but numb nonetheless.

"Ona, you're smart. You know nothing in this world is free. All the extras this ship's been unrolling for us? You've been paying for them under the table. Well, under the sheets might be more correct."

"Hey! I haven't been in bed with ship staff, you ass."

"Yeah, okay, Ona. That's technically true. Riker Ewan doesn't work for Stewart-Russ Cruise Line. But since he's Kate Russ's son, the technicalities aren't all that important."

Ona stumbled over her chair but didn't fall. She whipped around to Riker. "Your family owns this ship? You said you work in your father's bar."

"He told you that?" Cole said into the microphone. "Good thing I checked into this for you, Stilts. Your marine and his father do operate a bar in Boston, Massachusetts. But Riker *owns* that property. His mother's the Russ in Stewart-Russ. She was slumming it with a blue-collar barkeep, just like Riker was slumming it with you this entire week. In case anyone can't connect the dots, she wasn't really seeing the guy."

Riker stood, cupped her head. "Ona, I wanted to talk to you—"

Cole approached them, downing the champagne. "So

you're not wondering later," he said to Riker, "I saw the number on your phone when you got that call in the bar. I heard your side of the conversation and, gotta say, the research was a hell of a fun way to kill a few hours." He had the nerve to touch Ona's back, and she flinched. "Now, Stilts, don't take it out on me. I asked you to join me at the top. The offer's off the table."

Ona bolted. She'd been exposed as a fake and a fool. All those lies… There were too many, and they smothered her. Finding it difficult to run, she grabbed the bottom of her dress. Why had she bought this dress? Why had she thought she could pretend her way to a career she could make her own? Why had she let herself love another liar?

"You said I could see you alone," Riker said behind her.

Where he'd come from, she didn't know, and it didn't matter.

"That was before I found out you've been lying. This isn't fate and we're not meant to be. You targeted me and I let myself fall for it."

"I didn't target you!"

"You did!" Ona's shrill voice rang out and she took an abrupt turn around a corner and tugged open a colossal door. A sauna. No, it was a sparse yet luxurious room containing a pool filled with bubbly. Great—a champagne pool. Running inside, she reprimanded herself for not being wiser than this. And because she heard him still tight on her trail, she shouted, "I'm done with love. I'm done with liars!"

Riker secured her shoulders, turned her. "You lied, Ona. You lied about your job. You weren't real with me, either."

"It's not the same," she protested. "You made me think

we were the same. You had me believing we were friends and this was meant to be. Damn it, you had me thinking I was insane for loving you, but going with it anyway because my heart said it was right."

"Bullshit. No one makes you do what you don't want to do. You wanted to think we're friends and you wanted to love me. I didn't demand that from you." His hands flexed on her shoulders and his glare made it impossible for her to blink. "Know what, now that it's out there, I'm going to demand it. I want that from you."

"You're not getting anything more than what you've already gotten. Hope it was good for you."

"It was," he said severely. "It *is* good."

Still clasping her with one hand, he brought them to the edge of the pool and plunged in. A wave of champagne splashed the floor and Ona's dress, but before she could reel back, he hauled her into the pool with him. Her gown billowed. Millions of bubbles surfaced. She sputtered, pinching her nose to ease the stinging tickle of the champagne.

The pool smelled of celebration and recklessness. Swimming through the liquid, she met him with a retaliatory shove. "That was for my dress." Another push, this time with both hands, and it brought him flush against one wall of the pool. "That was for my hair."

"What else? There's something else, right? Has to be." Champagne dripped down the sides of his face. How many kisses would it take to get her drunk?

But this wasn't about kisses or love. She had to make her body remember that. "You lied to me. Nothing I do will change that."

"I did lie. You lied, too."

"I pretended to not be a failure. I pretended to fit in with my peers. And I shouldn't have pretended to be a seasoned event planner when I'm just starting out professionally, but that's a beef between PAAC and me, and between the glee club and me. It has nothing to do with you."

"Okay, Ona. Here are my crimes. Everything I told you about me and Boston and the marines and the bar back home is the truth. But I screwed up when I omitted that Kate Russ is my mother. I did that because of a business situation that's between Kate and me, and I've been feeling terrible about it since that first day." He stretched out his arms as though to taunt, "Take your next strike."

"All those courtesies the whole cruise? Those weren't courtesies, were they? They were compensation, right? Because you knew you'd end up having sex with me? That's the way Cole put it."

Riker swore. "Cole saw that he lost something he wanted to win, and he attacked. Guest Services wanted to keep you happy so you wouldn't hop on some mission to prove the mistake wasn't your fault."

"When did you find out?"

"That first day, after you left Sirens' Song."

For six days he'd withheld the truth. "Letting me take the fall so you could protect your mama's company? That's despicable."

"I wasn't out to protect the company, Ona. I was getting what I need to start shutting things down, starting with this ship."

She shook her head. "That's not any better!" Swallowing, struggling to think past the thick webs of hurt, she said, "I want a direct answer. Did you, Riker, order any of those favors?"

"The ballroom," he said. "And it wasn't a trade-off for sex. It was something I figured would put a smile on your face. It did. You smiled and you had this look that said, 'I'm freakin' proud of myself.' And it was so damn amazing to see you like that."

"Except it was a lie. Everything about us is a lie."

"What you just said was a lie," he flung back at her. "There's some truth between us. Find it, Ona, and tell me if that's enough to get us through this. 'Cause now we *are* fighting, and I don't wanna fight with you."

Ona threw herself into his kiss, surrendering to a tearless sob as she pulled angrily at his shirtfront. The champagne made her clumsy, but she wouldn't stop. When she got his shirt unbuttoned she went immediately to open his pants. With the other hand she gripped the back of his head.

"My body's never lied to you, Ona. I've wanted you every day since I saw you on the other side of that glass tower." His kiss was champagne-flavored and spiced with regret. "I didn't know you before that. I wasn't right before that."

She watched desire seep into his silvery-blue irises as his flesh swelled in her fist—but it wasn't enough. She needed more.

His hands found her breasts through her soaked gown, and his voice filled her ears with promises that were no doubt dirty and apologies that were no doubt sincere. But still she needed more.

Ona released his erection, turned and gripped the edge of the pool. She felt him drag her gown up to the pool's surface, and when his legs nudged hers apart, she was hungry to have him inside her. She met his thrusts with harsh grinding, gasped in rhythm with his flesh entering and retreating as it built to an orgasm that shook his body and hers, too.

Stroking her spine, he slowed the pace but moved

deeper into her. When he brought a hand around her hip to stimulate her, she yelled out a moan. Covering his hand with one of hers, she closed her eyes and breathed until she melted in the pool.

Sloshing champagne everywhere, they climbed up over the edge of the pool and he kissed her.

"I—I can't," she whispered. "It's not enough. Sex isn't enough."

"And love? That ain't enough, either?"

"No." Hugging herself, Ona listened to his heavy footsteps leave the room.

"That is one big-assed basket."

Carrying the basket with two arms, Ona bumped her fanny against the rental car's door and prayed that the guy who'd spoken wasn't waiting on the other side of the basket with a paring knife. Though artistically wrapped in cellophane, the basket was stuffed beyond capacity with gourmet meats, crackers, cheese spreads and chocolates. It was also wrapped with satin ribbons that fluttered in the spring wind and made it impossible for Ona to see anything directly in front of her.

It didn't help that it was also after midnight. But when Ona had assured PAAC's headmaster and special activities council that she would right away personally deliver the customary venue host thank-you gift, she'd intended to keep her word.

Right away meaning about five and a half hours later, which was how long Ona had spent chauffeuring a multi-thousand-dollar food basket from Philadelphia to Boston. Pint's had a two o'clock closing time, so she wasn't worried about arriving at a locked door.

What she *was* a tad—all right, a ton—worried about was both she and her academy's basket being turned away at the doorway. When she'd stepped off *The Lure* in Miami, she hadn't gone to New York. She'd made her way to Philadelphia and had met with the school to confess her deception and general stupidity.

But the school officials had enlightened her that Kate Russ of Stewart-Russ Cruise Line had beat her to the academy—and had assumed full responsibility for the scheduling error. Compensating the academy with a profanely generous donation and a discounted group stay on any one of her company's ships, the woman had also illustrated a list of favorable reviews curiously posted by guests bearing the same initials as twenty of the people in PAAC's glee club group.

Mollified, the academy hadn't taken action against Ona for misrepresenting herself as a professional event planner.

"We aren't in the habit of hiring amateurs to coordinate our events," the headmaster had said in that frank growl that might intimidate most who hadn't grown up in the sketchy parts of town. "Now that you are a paid professional, PAAC hopes you'll consider joining the committee for the full class reunion this summer and working with us on a few other social functions. Think about it. Oh, and Ms. Tracy—try to stay out of trouble."

Riker Ewan wasn't expecting her. She'd thought it best to not give him time to skip out of the bar or the city—not that she could fairly blame him for preferring to avoid her. She had been stubborn, deaf to his explanations and reasoning, and blind to the burn of love that bonded them, and she wouldn't go away just because she figured it might be easier to never love again.

He'd tried for her—for them. She hadn't. And now she was in his town because she'd been wrong before.

Love was enough. At least it was enough to compel

her to hear him out and to try to see the situation from that of a position other than victim. When it came to love, Ona had always played the victim. It was time to retire that role.

"Where you towing that?" the guy in front of her asked, and Ona imagined how ridiculous she must look buckling under the bulky thing.

"Pint's."

"I know the place."

"Know Riker Ewan?"

"Yeah, I do." A big pair of calloused hands came around the sides of the basket and lifted away from Ona's grip. Narrow brown eyes that reminded her of warm cocoa and a cozy fire greeted her. A sharp grin had the grizzled guy's face cracking into dozens of fine wrinkles. "I'm his dad. Emory."

"Oh! I—I'm Ona Tracy."

Emory Ewan nodded, shifting his jaw from side to side. "Uh-huh."

"I met Riker on a cruise."

"*Yeah*, you did." The man jerked his chin toward the brick building in front of them. "Riker doesn't talk if he doesn't wanna. He wanted to talk about you."

Ona wasn't sure if she should squeal or cringe. What she and Riker had done on *The Lure* wasn't something you wrote about on a postcard…or discussed in barkeep chats with your father.

Emory escorted her into the bar, and Ona's gaze bounced around the space. Muted lights, easy music, clean tables, mahogany bar, pool table, wooden stools. A mechanical bull wearing a tricorn hat and a sign that read You Are Out of Order.

A decent-sized flat-screen was mounted on a wall,

but *Diff'rent Strokes* on the small tube television behind the bar drew her attention.

"From the 1950s through the 1980s," Emory said, pointing at the television set. "The best TV you're ever gonna see, sweetheart. Guess that was before your time."

"I grew up on reruns," she told him, smiling as she remembered her conversation with Riker.

"Thank your parents, then." Emory winked then hollered, "Son, got a delivery here. It's the biggest damn basket I've ever seen. It's got food."

At the word *food*, the strands of folks around the pool and at the bar snapped alert.

Ona stood in front of the bar, nibbling her lip as she saw him come from a back room carting a box of pint glasses. "I brought the basket." *Whoa, was that lame! Didn't PAAC tell you what to say?* "I mean, on behalf of the Philadelphia Academy of Arts and Culture, I'm happy to present this small token of gratitude for your generosity in hosting our event. Please accept this basket with our heartfelt thanks."

"That's very formal of you, Philly," Riker said, setting down the box and dragging a bar towel off his shoulder.

"It's printed on the card, and the headmaster signed it." She looked into his eyes and found him to be as closed off as she'd ever seen him. "Um…now that that's done, I should be heading back."

"At 12:40?"

"Yeah, Riker. What's for me in Boston?"

Emory cleared his throat. "Son, I'm going to get back to the house. I don't think all these folks would make a stink if you opened this basket and sent them on their way so you can close up a little early tonight." He sent

Ona a friendly smile. "If he can talk you out of driving all night, the apartment upstairs is fit for a lady."

As Riker and his father doled out free food to their lingering patrons, Emory put on a faded cap and left, and Riker locked the bar behind him.

"So, nobody left but you and me," he said, leaning over the bar. "And classic TV and what's left in that basket."

"And the mechanical bull." Her smile was weak. "I didn't drive five hours for the basket, Riker. I drove because the words on the side of our ship said *Omnia Vincit Amor.* Love conquers all. Love *is* enough to help me try to get past what happened."

"Then let me tell you something Cole didn't find out. Emory Ewan's not my father. Not biologically."

"He's not?"

"Nah. Kate and Emory had a fling. She *wanted* him to be my father, so she made it so—until I got hurt in Afghanistan and found out the DNA didn't add up right."

Ona touched his hand. "Do you know who—"

"Yeah." Riker started to wipe the bar. "Let's just say that a cruise line isn't the only thing that John Alison Stewart and Kate Russ share."

Damn. "Oh, Riker…"

"Lies are the foundation of my life, Ona. But I'm thinking it's time to stop letting that map out my future. So I dropped my mission to shut down Kate's ships. But I'm not about to go manage her company, either."

"What will you do?"

"I don't know. In the immediate future I'm going to finish closing Pint's for the night. As for the sort-of-immediate future, the Red Sox are at Fenway this weekend. What are my chances of getting you to a game?"

"I don't have set-in-stone weekend plans, so I'd say good. PAAC re-upped me for reunion committee—the full class reunion. A formal thing in August. I was thinking this time I'd bring my real lover. I was thinking you might be up for it?"

"I might." He came around the bar, pinioning her. "You owe me a cheesesteak."

"Right. I should make good on that."

"You will, but it can wait." Riker's sexy, dangerous mouth finally found its way back to where it belonged—against hers. "Right now, Ona, I just want you."

* * * * *

REQUEST YOUR FREE BOOKS!

2 FREE NOVELS
PLUS 2 *FREE GIFTS!*

KIMANI™
ROMANCE

Love's ultimate destination!

YES! Please send me 2 FREE Harlequin® Kimani™ Romance novels and my 2 FREE gifts (gifts are worth about $10). After receiving them, if I don't wish to receive any more books, I can return the shipping statement marked "cancel." If I don't cancel, I will receive 4 brand-new novels every month and be billed just $5.44 per book in the U.S. or $5.99 per book in Canada. That's a savings of at least 16% off the cover price. It's quite a bargain! Shipping and handling is just 50¢ per book in the U.S. and 75¢ per book in Canada.* I understand that accepting the 2 free books and gifts places me under no obligation to buy anything. I can always return a shipment and cancel at any time. Even if I never buy another book, the two free books and gifts are mine to keep forever.

168/368 XDN GH4P

Name _____ (PLEASE PRINT)

Address _____ Apt. #

City _____ State/Prov. _____ Zip/Postal Code

Signature (if under 18, a parent or guardian must sign)

Mail to the **Reader Service:**

IN U.S.A.: P.O. Box 1867, Buffalo, NY 14240-1867
IN CANADA: P.O. Box 609, Fort Erie, Ontario L2A 5X3

Want to try two free books from another line?
Call 1-800-873-8635 or visit www.ReaderService.com.

* Terms and prices subject to change without notice. Prices do not include applicable taxes. Sales tax applicable in N.Y. Canadian residents will be charged applicable taxes. Offer not valid in Quebec. This offer is limited to one order per household. Not valid for current subscribers to Harlequin® Kimani™ Romance books. All orders subject to credit approval. Credit or debit balances in a customer's account(s) may be offset by any other outstanding balance owed by or to the customer. Please allow 4 to 6 weeks for delivery. Offer available while quantities last.

Your Privacy—The Reader Service is committed to protecting your privacy. Our Privacy Policy is available online at www.ReaderService.com or upon request from the Reader Service.

We make a portion of our mailing list available to reputable third parties that offer products we believe may interest you. If you prefer that we not exchange your name with third parties, or if you wish to clarify or modify your communication preferences, please visit us at www.ReaderService.com/consumerchoice or write to us at Reader Service Preference Service, P.O. Box 9062, Buffalo, NY 14240-9062. Include your complete name and address.

This summer is going to be hot, hot, hot
with a new miniseries
from fan-favorite authors!

YAHRAH ST. JOHN
LISA MARIE PERRY
PAMELA YAYE

HEAT WAVE OF DESIRE

Available June 2015

HOT SUMMER NIGHTS

Available July 2015

HEAT OF PASSION

Available August 2015

California Desert Dreams